# ADORABLE FAT GIRL IN LOCKDOWN

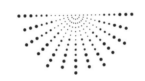

## BERNICE BLOOM

# A LETTER TO MY READERS

3rd May 2020

Dear reader,

This book has been written at a surreal moment in time, when the world is in lockdown and we are all forced to stay at home to avoid the spread of coronavirus. It's a serious time, when many people are worried either about themselves or their elderly relatives and it's a difficult time for many people who are at home alone and feel isolated. The daily announcements of the death toll from government ministers are both sad and worrying.

But it's also been a time of mischief and mayhem. A time when many people who would normally spend every waking hour at work are finding themselves with a more relaxed approach to life: waking at midday, eating whenever they want and watching Netflix series day and night.

It's been like that terrific but discombobulating time between Christmas and New Year when no one has any idea what day it is, what time it is, whether there's any post or whether the shops are open.

We are not supposed to go out unless we absolutely have to, but information is emerging that it's good to get outside because vitamin D, which comes from sunshine, helps to fight the disease, so we go out on our daily walks, tiptoeing through the streets like cat burglars, not entirely sure whether we should be there, not sure whether to acknowledge other people, and desperately trying to stay two metres away from everyone.

In time-honoured tradition, the way in which many of us have dealt with the developing situation is to drink unhealthy quantities, eat unhealthy quantities and buy lots of ridiculous things online. We're all sending funny memes to one another and reminiscing about a time when we could walk to the park, sit down on a bench and chat. Never have so many wanted so little. We've learned lots of new lingo as well: who'd ever heard of furlough before? And we have been able to look into the houses of all our colleagues during the interminable zoom meetings that puncture our days.

Now there are signs that the lockdown will soon be lifted, so I wanted to recall some of the daft things we've been through, and who better to guide us than mad Mary Brown - the plump and beautiful star of the Adorable Fat Girl series of books.

I really hope you enjoy the story, but most of all I hope that you and your family are well and are enjoying dressing in the pink feather boas, orange capes and green, plastic boots that you bought from eBay after that second bottle of Sauvignon. Stay safe, everyone, and thank you so much for buying my book

BB xxx

# THE STORY SO FAR...

The story so far...

The Adorable Fat Girl books can easily be read as stand-alone stories, but if you are reading them in order, this is where we were as the last one ended...

At the end of the last book (*Adorable Fat Girl & the Six-week Transformation*), Mary Brown was preparing for Charlie's 30th birthday party where she hoped to bump into Ted, her ex-boyfriend, with whom she is still in love.

But then coronavirus hit.

The world closed down.

Charlie's party was postponed, and as this book opens, Mary is spending lockdown in her flat with Juan, the glamorous Spanish dancer who she met on a cruise and who has come over to stay with her. She has been furloughed from her job, and is whiling away the days, as we all are, waiting for lockdown to end.

# CHAPTER ONE

"*H*ave you seen the biscuits?" I say, as Juan stretches out against the back of the sofa like a languid, hairless cat. He is wearing a crop top (yes, I know, I've tried telling him) and jeans. Who wears jeans anymore? I haven't been out of my pyjamas since Boris looked into the camera with hitherto unseen earnestness, and told us all to stay in our homes.

I think the world divided into two at that point... half the world (my half) thought - oh joy - no more jeans! I can stay inside all day and mooch around in leggings and pyjamas. The other half (Juan's half) thought, as they ironed their jeans, that they would dress just as well in lock-down as at any other time. These people have been spending their time being productive and healthy and doing on-line Pilates lessons, learning how to grow their own steamed kale and thatch a roof. I've been eating and drinking.

"I saw the empty biscuit packet in the bin earlier," says Juan, arching his back like no normal person should be able to. "I think you must have finished them."

"Damn. Have I finished them already? I'm sure there aren't as many in the packet as there used to be. Do you think they are putting fewer biscuits into them in lock-down? I seem to be going through them at a tremendous rate."

Juan raises his eyebrows at me (he hasn't been able to get Botox since the lockdown began, so he can do facial expressions now). "I don't know about the number of biscuits in a pack, but you are certainly going through them at a tremendous rate."

"But you're allowed to in lockdown. The calories don't count. Did you not realise?"

"I had no idea, Mary. Coronavirus kills calories, does it?"

"Exactly."

I am on furlough from my job at *Fosters Gardening and DIY Centre,* and I'm using my time efficiently and brilliantly to catch up on everything that Netflix has ever produced, and to eat everything in sight. I've been through all the box-sets I meant to watch but never had the time. I've seen the whole of *Suits, The Affair* and *Game of Thrones.* Now I'm in the process of re-watching every single episode of *Sex and the City.* My God it's good. The clothes! New York! I'm also consuming more biscuits than any other human being ever while watching it.

"I think I've tried every biscuit in the world now," I say. "I might go onto cake."

"Or you could try learning a new language, or come to some of my on-line Pilates classes?"

"I could," I say. "But it's best to be careful while coronavirus is knocking around."

"Eh?"

"Well, if I get injured doing Pilates, what will happen? I'll have to go into hospital for treatment and I'll pick up the virus and die."

Juan shakes his head. "We could learn a new language together?" he suggests. "It would be good to come out of lock-down having achieved something."

"No, no, no," I say. "You're missing the whole point of lock-down. This is a special moment in time when we all just relax and retreat into lives of chocolate and tv. If you want us to do something together, how about we eat cake together? We could try a different cake every day, and see which is the best. We could publish our results. It would be a valuable service."

"It doesn't sound that healthy. I'm trying to stay fit during lock-down."

"Well stop it. No good will come of being fit."

"I feel much better about myself when I'm fit," he says, articulating the essence of the differences between us. "I feel happy when I'm fitter."

"I understand that, but this is cake we're talking about here. You can't honestly believe that anything will make you happier than eating lots of cake. If you can, we can't be friends anymore; it's as simple as that."

"Ha. You're nuts. I like cake, angel, it's just - you know - I like other things too…"

"Hang on. I'VE GOT IT."

I've had a brain wave. It's the best idea ever.

"Let's do a World Cup of Cakes."

"A what? A World Cup of Cakes? How? I mean: why?"

"Because it would be brilliant, and a real achievement."

"Yeah, there are other things we could achieve though…

Charlie's learning Chinese, apparently, did you know that? And Shakespeare wrote King Lear during lock-down for the plague."

"Yeah, well Charlie's lost her mind and Shakespeare only wrote about some damn king called Lear because he never thought of doing a World Cup of Cakes. If he'd done a cake World Cup, we'd never have had to study those damn plays at school. I'd be much more interested in knowing whether carrot cake or Victoria sponge cake was better."

"Fair point," says Juan, standing up and lifting his leg out in front of him so high it almost touches his nose. In jeans!

"Human bodies shouldn't be able to do that."

"It's important that I keep fit. You should be joining me."

"I can't. I've got a World Cup to organise, and you should be helping me."

"I can't. I've got fitness to do, and you should be doing it with me."

"Oh God, Juan - but cakes are so much more fun than fitness. And I know that people all over the world are learning to crochet and teach their dogs to sing like Pavarotti, but a World Cup of Cakes would be brilliant. I'm going to trademark it. We could end up being rich and famous and have free cake for life."

Juan looks deeply unimpressed.

"OK," I say. "I will strike a deal with you: if I promise to do some of that keep fit rubbish with you, will you do a World Cup of Cakes with me?"

"OK," he says, reluctantly. "That sounds like a fair deal. But how would we do it?"

"Go out and buy a tonne of cakes and eat them," I say, with a shrug. "It's the simplest ideas that are the best."

"I mean - how do we share the results with the world? Or is this just an in-house cake competition?"

"Good heavens. No. The whole world needs to know about our cake tasting. We'll do a blog or something, shall we? That can't be too hard to do."

"Or videos on YouTube? That would be good fun. I could show off my buff pecs at the same time."

Juan drops into the press up position and lifts his arms into the air one at a time.

"Yes, top plan. I'll research it and come back when I know what's what."

"And, remember, you have to do some fitness work with me as well."

"I will, I will, I promise. Now leave it with me and I'll plan the greatest World Cup ever. Greater than the actual World Cup, because we'll be eating cake in ours and there will be no football!"

Little did I know on that quiet morning, as we chatted amiably in the kitchen, that something quite extraordinary was going to happen with my World Cup of Cakes, something neither of us could possibly have predicted...

# CHAPTER TWO

*I*t turns out that it's not that easy to trademark a World Cup of Cakes, but I'm going to start using the trademark sign anyway, whenever I remember, just to make the whole thing look more professional and sophisticated. I've been researching the whole thing for hours. If anyone looks at my Google search, they will think I've been abducted or something. I've spent all afternoon googling "World Cup" and "how does the football World Cup work?" For someone who has not the remotest interest in anything sporty (except for the thighs of those who play), it's a remarkable set of Google searches.

The good news is that I think I have the perfect format for my *World Cup of Cakes* ™ . Over the next four days, we will consume five cakes a day, and give them marks out of 10. The top two in each group will go through to the quarter-finals (so, eight cakes in the quarter-finals), then the winners of those quarter-finals will go through to the semi-finals, with the winners playing off in the grand final.

I rush into the sitting room from the World Cup planning office (my bedroom), waving sheets of A4 paper at Juan. "I've done it: we've got a format…"

He takes the pieces of paper from me and looks over them, and even though I say this myself, he looks pretty darn impressed.

"Wow, you've done this properly - like a proper World Cup," he says.

"It **IS** a proper World Cup."

"I know, but - I mean - really properly - this should be fun. Which cakes will we be eating first?"

"All in good time," I say. "We've got to do the draw to see which cakes fall into each group. We should really have a celebrity from the cake world to do the draw - you know, Mary Berry or someone like that, but it might have to be you and me."

"Yes, I think we can get away without a celebrity in a lock-down World Cup," he reassures me. "Perhaps in follow-up tournaments we can have Gordon Ramsay arriving to take the Victoria sponge out of its box or something."

"Good thinking."

"So, what are the timings of this, then? When do we start?"

"We're going to be starting tomorrow. There's no point in waiting a moment longer: Tuesday, Wednesday, Thursday and Friday are the pool games, then it's the quarter-finals on Saturday, semi-finals on Sunday and the World Cup final on Monday."

"You have spent more time researching this than I've ever seen you research anything."

"Well it's very important to me," I say, as I retreat back to my World Cup planning office to decide which cakes will feature in my inaugural tournament.

The first task facing me is getting my head around what constitutes a 'cake'. When does a cake become a biscuit and when does a cake become a pudding? It's not easy running a major international tournament.

I look into the mirror at my weary, makeup-less face as I consider the plight of the Jaffa cake and the sticky toffee pudding: are they cakes? But all I can really ascertain from staring at my reflection is that I need my hair doing so badly it's ridiculous. I like to kid myself that I am a natural golden blonde, but it turns out I'm not all that blonde without my regular highlights. At the moment I look like a badger. It's not a great look.

I decide to call Charlie on house party to see what she thinks about my cake idea, and also to find out whether she has any ideas about how you can sort your hair out in lockdown.

"I'm going to do a *World Cup of Cakes* ™," I say proudly when her familiar, beautiful face fills the screen. She has terrible black roots on show, so I decide not to seek hairdressing advice from her. At the mention of a *World Cup of Cakes* ™, her nose and eyebrows crunch together in confusion.

"You don't look impressed. Let me explain... I'm going to take 20 different cakes, taste them all, and the best ones will go through to the quarter-finals, then the semi-final, then the final."

"So, basically, you have worked out a way to justify eating a lot of cake over the next few days."

"Yeah."

"Excellent. Well that sounds like a jolly good plan. How can I help? Do you need help with the judging? I'm always available to eat cake."

"Well, yes, of course I'd love you to be involved in the judging, but we are in lockdown, so you can't. I really need your help choosing which cakes should be in the World Cup though."

"Pick the ones you like best?"

"I could do that, but if I do a list of the ones I like best, I'd have banoffee pie in there…does that sound like a cake? Is it a cake? Am I allowed pies, or must they have cake in the title in order to qualify, in which case I can definitely have Jaffa cake? What about things like cheesecake and carrot cake? I like both of those, but really – do cheese and carrot have any rightful place in the ingredients for a cake? It's very hard, Charlie."

"I can see it's hard. When are you planning to start?"

"Tomorrow, of course," I explain. "I need to get a list of all the cakes that will be competing, then go out and buy the first five."

"Well then, you better make sure you only pick cakes that are available. Remember that shops don't have stock like they used to."

"Good thought," I say. "That's why I brought you onto the executive committee, for this sort of sensible, practical thinking."

"I'm on the executive committee, am I? Excellent news."

"Yes, you are. I'm going to google all the different cakes available in Tesco's now and work out what to do. I'll keep you fully briefed."

"Zai jian," said Charlie, in what I take to be Chinese, and her face disappears from the screen.


I decide, in my great wisdom, that the best way to find out what's available in the cake aisle at Tesco's, is to go to the cake aisle and take a look. Juan says he's not coming to the supermarket with me because he wants to sit outside and watch the birds.

This has become an almost daily activity for him since lockdown. He takes scraps of food out there and watches them for ages. There are two pigeons who come regularly to feast on the cereal and bread that he throws out. His favourites are called Bertie and Winston both of whom have hooked beaks and white patches on the front of their faces to distinguish them from the others. He's convinced that the more he goes out there and talks to them, the friendlier they get. There's also a large crow that walks across the top of the guttering, kicking debris as it goes, so that odd stones fall into the garden just missing the feeding birds. The crow is like an angry teenager, kicking out randomly as he walks, so we've called him 'Kevin the teenager.'

"I'll see you later," I say to Juan and he salutes me from his chair in the tiny patio area outside the front of the building. He's staring at a pile of stale bread crumbs lying a couple of feet in front of him. If you didn't know him, you'd think he'd lost his mind.

It's weird walking through the streets during lockdown. I live in a busy part of the world, just outside London, in a town called Cobham. It's got a lively, vibrant centre to it with lots of bars and cafes, and the roads are always busy. Today there's hardly anyone around. One car passes me, and I find myself looking at the driver in an accusatory way. Should you really be out? Is your journey essential? I catch the driver's eye, and realise that he is looking at me too, presumably wondering exactly the same thing. Well, sir, yes – my journey is essential. I'm going to buy lots of cake.

I walk along the silent streets until I see Tesco ahead, and a small queue of people standing metres apart from one another waiting to go in. As I approach it, someone is walking towards me on my side of the street, it's quite a narrow pavement, and I don't think either of us knows quite what to do. I'm worried that if I walk into the road in a big loop to avoid her, it'll make it look as if I think she's carrying some terrible illness, but if we walk right past each other we certainly won't be keeping the recommended distance away. I don't want to get ill just when I'm about to organise a major international cake tournament. In the end I walk into the road and do the big loop, and the woman does look at me as if I'm slightly deranged.

A security guard stands on the door of Tesco's, making sure we all stand a distance apart from one another, and only enter the shop one by one. Is the strangest thing. On the news, we are used to seeing huge queues outside bakeries in Poland as they struggle to have enough food to go round, but we are very lucky in this country. Waiting to get into a supermarket is something we've never had to do. I come from a generation that has never had rationing to content with, or shortages at all. Now, though, we stand and queue.

Once I'm in the shop, I wander down the aisles that have been marked out with tape to ensure that everyone goes round the same way and there's the minimum amount possible of bumping into one another. There are only two loaves of bread left and I feel bad as I take one, but I need to have something in the house that's not full of sugar and coated in icing. Juan keeps feeding all our damn bread to the birds, so we're forever running out. There's no pasta at all on the shelves and no eggs. It's remarkable what sells out when there's a global pandemic: eggs, pasta and bread. There's some toilet paper there, so I take two packs of four toilet rolls before picking up speed as I motor on to the cake section... Lots of cakes. Thank goodness. To be honest, I'm surprised and delighted by the variety of cakes on offer, and pull out my notebook to list the ones that are there. In a way, it would be good to buy all the cakes now, so we've got them in the kitchen and can just sample five a day, without having to come out to the shops every morning, but it'll be difficult to carry them home. I decide that I will buy 15 now, and I will have to come back for another five.

Then I meander through the store, picking up a few basic essentials until I get to the hair dye. There are normally shelves and shelves of different hair dyes, root touch-ups and sprays of all kinds. Not now. Just around eight dyeing kits sit there. I offer a silent prayer that one of them is either honey or ash blonde. Of course, they're not. My silent prayers never work. Two of them are jet black and the others are various shades of auburn.

"Do you have any other hair dyes?" I ask a passing shop assistant.

"I assume you're looking for a light blonde colourant?" she says. "I'm afraid we don't. There are a couple more over there, by the hairspray, but I'm not sure any of them are for blonde hair."

I stride over to the hairsprays and see one hair dye, in a much lighter colour than the others, but still not my shade of blonde...it is sort of gingery blonde.

"That's the one," says the assistant, coming up beside me (two metres away...she's not insane). "How lucky to find one."

"Yes, but it's kind of ginger, isn't it?"

"It's strawberry blonde, but it's blonde really. It'll be fine on your hair."

I have to add that the assistant's hair is terrible. If she had beautiful, glossy, well-maintained hair in a gorgeous colour, I'd be more inclined to take her word, but I'm still not sure.

"Oh, you've got the last one. Damn. Are you definitely taking that?" asks another woman, peering over my shoulder (she's definitely not 2m away). She has gorgeous, stylish hair, roughly the same colour as mine.

"Yes, I am taking it," I say quickly, heading to the cashiers where I pile all my goods onto the little conveyor belt. I look at the dye again. It looks quite bright. What if it goes orange? I don't want carrot-coloured roots, that would be worse than dark roots. Perhaps I should put it back? I put it to one side while I unload the rest of my shopping: chocolate cake, coffee and walnut cake, Victoria sponge, banoffee p…

"Oh, hello."

In front of me stands Liz, the teacher who led the fat loss club that I went to a couple of years ago. She is a really lovely woman, and we stayed in touch for a while, as did a lot of us from the club, but as is always the case, we drifted apart eventually, and kind of lost touch.

"It's so lovely to see you," she says, half reaching out to hug me but then pulling away because she realises she's not allowed to come near me. No one knows the rules any more, do they? I know we're not supposed to hug, or kiss each other on the cheeks, but it's very hard to know what to do when you see someone you know but haven't seen for a while. In the end we both smile at each other and shrug.

"It's ridiculous not to be able to hug you," I say. "It's really lovely to see you."

"Yes, you too…"

"I'm just picking up a few essentials," I say, in a small talk sort of way, which is a huge mistake because it simply means that I am pointing out to her the enormous quantity of cake on the conveyor belt.

"Goodness, are you having a party?" she says.

"No," I reply. "It's just for this thing I'm doing: a kind of project."

"Oh, thank goodness for that. I thought you were going to eat them all."

"Well, I am. But it's all in the name of research."

"Right," says Liz, nodding in a way which clearly indicates that she doesn't think it's at all right.

"I was going to get in touch, actually," she says. "There is a new advanced course in weight management: I wondered whether you fancied coming to it. It starts in a couple of months, lots of the guys from the first course, the one that you were on, will be there."

I swear she looks at the cakes on the conveyor belt as she says this, as if to indicate that I need to get back down to fat club as fast as my little podgy legs can carry me.

"Of course, I'd love to come. It would be great to see everyone again."

"And to learn about healthy eating," she adds.

"Yes, of course. Well, that will be great. I better go and pay for this lot now, but it's lovely to see you."

"Yes, you too," says Liz, still unable to take her eyes off the 15 cakes I'm buying. "Make sure you tell Ted won't you. It would be great to see him there too."

"Yes," I say. "I will." And for a moment I feel very sad.

"So, are you not buying that then?" says the lady with the nice blonde hair, pointing at the hair dye and shaking me out of my thoughts.

"Yes." I knock it onto the conveyor belt alongside a pack of brownies and a black forest gateau. I am definitely going to buy it now, just to spite her.


Walking back I am in a bit of a daze. Bumping into the woman who runs Fat Club when you're buying 15 cakes isn't ideal. Neither is buying ginger hair dye just because someone else wants it.

As I walk down the High Street towards the flat, I'm feeling pretty low, which is unlike me, but the whole lock-down thing is getting to me a bit. Especially the fact that Ted's name has just been mentioned and now I feel all wistful and just wish I was back with him. I'm walking along, staring at the ground in a sulky manner, when in front of me, a few yards ahead, I see a rather forlorn-looking potato lying on the pavement. I stop and look at the lonely, discarded root vegetable, feeling overwhelmingly sad for it. I know it's only a potato but in that moment it is as if it were a child left abandoned on the side of the road after a picnic; the family having driven off and arrived home to their warm house while the child waits, hoping that someone kind will come and rescue it from an uncertain, but terrifying, future. It's a large, misshapen, ugly-looking thing that has started sprouting. Really the runt of potatoes: overweight, ungroomed and ugly. I feel very sorry for it, and I know that if I don't take the potato home, I will think about it, probably for months. Imagining it there, alone, going to waste, kicked and buffeted by passers-by. Unloved. No one should be unloved. So, I put my bags of cakes down and pick up the potato, smiling at it and stroking it gently. "You can come home with me, Mr Potato. I'm going to call you Peter. We will have cake," I said. Unfortunately, I don't see Liz walk past me, increasing her speed as she notices me chatting to a root vegetable. "I live in a nice flat, Peter the potato," I'm saying. "You'll get to meet Juan, he's lovely."

I arrive back at the flat, clutching the potato and bags of cakes, to be greeted by Juan standing at the door. Part of me thinks he's come out to meet our vegetable guest, but he's just come out to help me carry the bags. I blunder up to the door with about 10 stone of cake and relinquish it all with great pleasure.

"Guess who I bumped into? Liz - the woman who runs Fat Club."

"Where?"

"In Tesco's. She was buying fruit and all sorts of healthy things, and she looked at the mountain of cakes I was buying and told me I need to come to a new fat club session very soon."

"Didn't you tell her about the World Cup?"

"No, I just wanted her to go, so I didn't talk very much. She is very nice, but I just felt really awkward with 15 cakes in front of me. And she asked about Ted as if I was still going out with him which was horrible."

Juan helps me to unload the bags and I put Peter the potato in his new home: the second cutlery draw in which I keep the wooden spoons, spatulas and 'stuff'. I take out the potato peeler in case he gets scared.

Juan is still wide-eyed as he regards the vast array of cakes before him.

"I only bought 15, and that was quite expensive," I say, shutting the cutlery drawer so Peter can go to sleep. "I'll need to go back and get another five for the final day, but we've got enough here for the next three days."

"You're taking this very seriously."

"Yes, well, it's cake. It deserves to be taken seriously."

"And you have to do some fitness work with me, you remember that, don't you?"

"Yes, of course. No problem at all. I'm looking forward to it. We will get onto that really soon. Now I've got to go and make a list of all the cakes and then we can do the draw for which group each of the cakes is going to go into, and tomorrow we are ready to start with the opening of the tournament. Do you think we should have an opening ceremony, like they do at the Olympics?"

"I don't know," says Juan. He is staring into the carrier bag as he talks to me. "Why have you bought bright ginger hair dye?"

"Because someone else wanted it."

"Right. I suppose that makes sense."


We sit down that evening to watch the daily press conference and to learn how many deaths there have been that day. Truly, it's the most depressing, but somehow unmissable, moment of the day. The medical and science people walk out, looking like they have the weight of the world on their shoulders, and the politicians come out and update us on how Boris Johnson is doing in intensive care. I watch it with morbid fascination. They are telling us today about the number of children who have died from the disease: it's the worst news. It all reminds me of an article I once read about aid workers having to bury all the bodies they had found after an earthquake.

"The smallest coffins are the hardest to lift," one of them said. That's stayed with me. I wish this horrible illness would just go away.

# CHAPTER THREE

t's Tuesday morning, but not any Tuesday morning. This is the day that the *World Cup of Cakes* ™ begins. Clearly we should have an opening ceremony of some sort, so I put two bottles of wine and a sparkling wine that's been in the kitchen cupboard for God knows how long into the fridge (I genuinely don't know how long, because I didn't know it was there, if I'd known it was there I'd have drunk it!)

I also need to dye my hair today, so I don't have a horrible black streak when millions of viewers tune in to see us launching the World Cup.

I could also do with going to the Post Office at some stage. I have so many parcels to send back. The postman arrived earlier with another pile of rubbish that I'd ordered online. I get so excited when I order things. I picture in my head how wonderful I will look, strolling down the street in lime trousers and pink high heels, clutching a designer handbag in the shape of a pair of scissors, then I place my orders with gusto. I always order these sorts of things after watching too much Sex and the City, and I think I live in Manhattan with Carrie and Samantha. But then the parcels arrive and I realise I've ordered a handbag in the shape of a pair of scissors. Why would anyone want a handbag in that shape?

The clothes I buy are invariably too small (in case you're wondering - they don't make lime green trousers above a size 14, but I convinced myself that they might fit anyway. unsurprisingly: they don't. In truth, I can barely get my ankles into them). The pink shoes are wonderful, but colossally high.

They will have to go back. I'm on first name terms with the guys in Cobham Post Office now (Pam and Raj) but they are the most miserable people on God's sweet earth, so I avoid going there whenever possible. This means that some of the parcels lie on my bedroom floor for a considerable amount of time. By the end of lockdown, I'll have enough stuff on my floor to open a hypermarket.

Juan seems perplexed by all the parcels arriving and he finds it wildly amusing when he hears the tear of Sellotape, then the sight of me heading off to the post office on the

High Street with a large bag of parcels. He keeps telling me to 'just stop buying shit.' Yeah, yeah, yeah. That's so easy to say, but desperately hard to do. Buying shit and eating shit are getting me through lockdown, and I know I'm not alone.

So, the parcels are lying on the floor, as a painful reminder of my recklessness with money, and I now I need to step over them, promising myself that I'll deal with them later, and go and wake up Juan so we can do the draw. Once that's done, I can put together a proper World Cup plan.

I knock on Juan's bedroom door and he opens it straight away, causing me to jump back a little bit. I assumed he'd be asleep but he's wide awake. He's wearing a purple crop top and purple leggings with sequins up the side.

"Is that the outfit you're wearing for the video today?" I say, thinking that the incredibly tight leggings will probably get us hundreds of extra views, but might be in breach of every single public decency law.

"What video?"

"What do you mean – what video? Today is the day that we launch the *World Cup of Cakes* ™."

"Oh, yes."

"You'd forgotten, hadn't you?"

"Well, yes, to be honest. I'm dressed like this because I was going to have a zoom chat with Gilly. I wasn't sure whether you were serious. Are you really going to make videos of you and me eating cake?"

"Absolutely I am. Do you want to zoom with your boyfriend first?"

"No, don't worry: I'll talk to him later."

"OK then, the first thing we need to do is the official draw. We're not going to put this onto video, but we are going to do it formally and seriously so that no one can accuse us of cheating.

"If one of the cakes complains that they are in a tough group and suspect foul play, then we will be called to the International Cake Council to explain ourselves. We need to be beyond reproach."

"Sure," he says. "Just a couple of things, though, first of all - cakes don't talk, so they are unable to lodge much of a complaint. Second - there is no International Cake Council. You just made that up."

"I might have," I agree. "Or it might just be a very secretive organisation that no one's ever heard of."

"One other thing, Mary. Who do you think all these people are who are going to watch the video?"

"Trust me," I say, without too much confidence. "This will be the greatest video ever. Now put some clothes on that make you look like a normal person, and let's get on with the draw."

I wander into the kitchen, and pour out two large glasses of sparkling wine. We don't need breakfast. It's 10 am, and the draw will be followed by cake eating, and the last thing we want it's to be full up before the competition starts. All we need is a little lubrication to get us through the morning.

Juan reappears in slightly more sober clothing and I hand him a beige-coloured felt bag. It's the one that my new handbag came in.

"Hold this." I say. He peers inside it.

"What are all these pieces of paper scrunched up for?"

"Each of those has the name of a cake on it, and you are going to draw them out and we're going to create the *World Cup of Cakes* ™."

"Right."

"But first, here: cheers!"

I hand him a glass of sparkling wine and he looks at me slightly dubiously. "Isn't it too early for drinking?"

"Nope. This is an international tournament, and it's bound to be drinking time somewhere. We can't exclude the people on the other side of the world. Have a taste."

"Actually, it's not bad. What is this?"

I take a closer look at the bottle, explaining to Juan that I've had it in the cupboard for ages.

"Oh, it's champagne!"

"Yum. No wonder it tastes so good. Perhaps we better just

have one glass of this, then go onto the wine, then come back to the champagne to have with the cakes when we're on air?"

"Is that how they do it in the real World Cup?" asked Juan.

"I imagine that's exactly how they do it. Now, we're going to draw out the cakes for Group A. Can you take a piece of paper please?"

Juan pulls out Victoria sponge cake, and listens as I perform a running commentary: "A lovely simple cake to start us off, the delicious Victoria sponge cake, popular amongst the elderly, is the first cake in Group A. Another cake please, Juan."

The next one out is Eckles cake.

"Very controversial," says Juan. "Why did you pick Eccles cakes? Are they even really cakes?"

"I had this conversation with myself yesterday, and I've decided they are cakes. And the reason they are in the competition is because they were in stock in Tesco's. If you want to change them for something else, you'll have to go out and buy something to replace them. Any more questions?"

"None at all. It seems like a fine choice. Shall I draw the next one?"

Next one out the bag is cheesecake. We have a blackcurrant cheesecake, largely because that was the only one they had in the shop. Next comes chocolate cake followed by lemon drizzle cake.

"Lemon drizzle cake is my favourite," says Juan.

"What is wrong with you? Have you no taste at all? You need cakes with thick icing, chocolate and joy. Lemon drizzle cake doesn't stand a chance. It's like you've got no idea about proper cake consumption."

Juan just shrugs. I don't think he was expecting to be

scolded quite so vehemently for expressing a simple preference. He has no idea how seriously I take cakes.

Group B is up next, Juan pulls out fondant fancies first. We have quite a discussion about whether they should qualify. Juan thinks they shouldn't.

"You know the rules: if you feel strongly about it, then you have to go out and find a replacement."

Juan rethinks his stance and agrees with me that the fondant fancy is indeed a very worthy competitor in the tournament. Next is fruit cake, gingerbread cake, Jaffa cakes and finally coffee and walnut cake.

"I'm not going to comment on the controversy of including Jaffa cakes," says Juan. "I know what you'll say - I'll have to go out and buy replacements. But I think you'll find the millions of people watching the tournament this afternoon will have something to say about it."

"Well, if it becomes too much of a controversy, I will release a statement, like they do in World Cups when someone fails a drugs test, or is in trouble in some way. In fact, I might have a red and yellow card system for cakes that are controversial."

"Right," says Juan and I can tell that he wishes he'd kept his mouth shut.

Group C contains sticky toffee pudding, banoffee pie, Battenberg cake, birthday cake and red velvet cake.

"Sticky toffee pudding?" says Juan in his ill-advised way. "How is sticky toffee pudding a cake?"

"Juan - I've explained a million times: these are cakes because they are all that was in the shop."

"OK."

"That Group C is quite magical," I say, as I write the different contenders down on a piece of paper. Sticky toffee pudding against red velvet cake, now there is a real battle for glory. I think that is what the football pundits would call the group of death."

Juan picks out the final contenders, so we have Christmas cake, chocolate brownie, black forest gateau, carrot cake and caterpillar cake in the final group.

"That completes the draw for the 2020 *World Cup of Cakes* ™. The competition will begin at 1pm with the cakes in Group A competing for the first quarter final place. Group B will be tomorrow, Wednesday. Group C is on Thursday and Group D is on Friday. Thank you for watching."

"You remember that we're not recording this, don't you?" says Juan. "Which is a bit of a shame because you sounded very professional there."

"Perhaps a new career beckons?" I try.

"Perhaps," he replies. "Cheers."

We raise our glasses to toast the *World Cup of Cakes* ™, then I put the champagne in the fridge, and we fill our glasses with wine.

"Can you help me dye my hair, before our live broadcast?" I ask Juan.

"Sure, but I've never done it before."

"It doesn't matter. My roots are coming through, I look ridiculous."

"You look fine."

"I'll look much better with my roots done."

"That's not guaranteed."

"Yes, it is. You'll be great."

"Mmmmm...I really hope so, but it might look a hell of a lot worse."

"I'll take that risk," I say, as I tip the contents of the box out and hand the instructions to Juan. "Nothing can go wrong; I just want you to do the roots. I'm sure you can manage that."

"Yeah, I'll try, I don't really know what I'm doing."

"That's what the instructions are for, now – get to it."

Juan fiddles around putting on the plastic gloves and mixing up the solutions, before painting it tentatively onto my parting. "You just want me to do the roots?"

"Yes, do the roots, then just run it all the way through and leave it on for a couple of extra minutes before washing it off."

"It's very orange," he says, but I tell him not to worry. It's too late now.

Juan takes a big sip of his wine, and continues. "You have a lot of roots here," he says. "Do I have to do all of them? The ones underneath as well?"

"Course you have to do all of them or I'll just look ridiculous."

He paints away, whistling to himself as he lifts up pieces of hair and deposits the dye. Soon it's all done and he is in the kitchen rinsing out the equipment he's used and setting a timer. "Imagine if it looks really good," he says. "Maybe I could introduce hairdressing to my portfolio. Come and do Pilates with Juan and get a free haircut."

"Yep, that would certainly work," I say.

It seems like no time at all (two glasses of wine) until the timer pings and it's time to wash out the dye. Juan makes me bend over the bath, while he inexpertly runs the shower over my head, soaking all my clothes and getting water all over the bathroom in the process.

"You're going to have to work on that technique if you're going to do this professionally," I comment. Then he wraps a towel around my head and tells me the job is done. He follows me as I walk into my bedroom and sit in front of the dressing table.

I remove the towel and peer into the mirror. "It doesn't look any different."

I peer more closely and part my hair with my fingers. The dark roots are slightly lighter, but it's really hard to tell when it's wet. So, I pull out my hairdryer and drop my head upside down, drying it off. When I fling my head back up again and look into the mirror it's not the greatest look in the world. He's not going to trouble Vidal Sassoon, that's for sure.

"My roots are orange!"

"That's not my fault," says Juan. "That's the colour you bought."

"But the picture on the box was of a woman with gorgeous honey blonde hair."

"The woman on the front has ginger hair."

"No – that's honey blonde. Are you blind?"

Then I see the look of fear and disappointment on Juan's face and relent. "I think ginger roots are better than dark roots, they won't show up so much when we are doing the World Cup later," I say. "Thank you for doing it."

"That's OK," says Juan, dismally, as he heads back to his room, leaving me in the World Cup Planning Office to write my speech for the opening of the *World Cup of Cakes* ™."

# CHAPTER FOUR

*O*K, so it would be a lie to say this is going as smoothly as I hoped it would. My hair is nowhere near as "OK" as I thought it was when Juan first dyed it. The roots are quite bright ginger, and the rest of the hair is blonde, but more reddish blonde than it was before. I do look very odd. Because of that I've drunk quite a lot, and now I've had so much wine that the hair isn't bothering me as much as it should. Poor Juan, who has also been drinking all day because he's mortified at what he's done to me, is also very drunk, and is refusing to look at my hair.

Somehow, in this condition, we are trying to work out how we put a video on YouTube. It's currently 12.50pm. We are due to start at 1pm, and Juan is filling up my glass. "Come on," he says, his eyes cast downwards so as to avoid looking at my ginger roots. "We can do this."

. . .

"Ladies and gentlemen and welcome to the first ever *World Cup of Cakes* ™, hosted by me – Mary Brown – and my glamorous assistant Juan Pedro."

"I'm more than just an assistant though," slurs Juan. "I'm also a hairdresser, and look what I did to her roots. Show them, Mary. I can't look, but you show the lovely viewers."

I bend my head over so that the ludicrous orange stripe is fully on show.

"I feel terrible," slurs Juan. "I have given her a terrible ginger stripe through the centre of her hair that is exactly the same colour as Donald Trump."

"It is," I say, looking again. "It's the colour of Donald's cheeks. And, for the avoidance of doubt, that wasn't the look I was going for."

Juan sighs deeply and drops his head into his hands.

"So, without further ado, let's get on with the tournament. Here, ladies and gentlemen, is the plan for the 2020 *World Cup of Cakes* ™."

I hold up the tournament plan so all of the viewers can see it...


GROUP A
Victoria Sponge Cake
Eccles Cake
Cheesecake
Chocolate cake
Lemon Drizzle Cake



GROUP B

Fondant Fancy
Fruit Cake
Gingerbread Cake
Jaffa Cakes
Coffee & Walnut Cake


GROUP C
Sticky Toffee Cake
Banoffee Pie Cake
Battenberg Cake
Birthday Cake
Red Velvet Cake


GROUP D
Christmas Cake
Brownie
Black Forest Gateau
Carrot Cake
Caterpillar Cake


QUARTER FINALS (Saturday)
WINNER OF A v RUNNER-UP IN B
WINNER OF B v RUNNER-UP IN A
WINNER OF C v RUNNER-UP IN D
WINNER OF D v RUNNER-UP IN C

SEMI FINALS (Sunday)
WINNER OF 1 v WINNER OF 4
WINNER OF 2 v WINNER OF 3

THIRD PLACE PLAY-OFF (Sunday)
LOSER OF A v LOSER OF B

FINAL (Monday)
WINNER OF A v WINNER OF B

"As you can see, we've got some incredible entries into this year's tournament. Group C is definitely the Group of Death, with sticky toffee and red velvet cake having to fight with birthday cake. It will be fascinating to see how that one turns out. Make sure you tune in on Thursday to have a look at that. So, I'll leave the World Cup groups up for just a second longer, then we will get on with the tasting for Group A."

"Do you want to say anything?" I ask Juan.

"No," he says, shaking his head.

"OK, ladies and gentlemen so you've seen the tournament schedule. Just to remind you of the rules: a slice of each cake will be consumed by the two judges, that is Juan and me. We will assess the cakes and award a mark to each. The two top cakes in each group will go through to the finals. The judges' decisions are final. No correspondence will be entered into. If you don't like our *World Cup of Cakes* ™, go and do one of your own.

"Right, on that note, the first cake we have here is Victoria sponge cake."

I reach into the drawer and pull out a knife, smiling at Peter the Potato as I do so, then I cut the Victoria sponge cake and produce two large slices. I hand a plate to Juan with one of the slices on and he takes a huge bite out of it straight away. I do the same. We are both absolutely starving, having not eaten all morning and drunk the best part of two bottles of wine. The cake tastes nice, but nothing special. I convey this to the viewer, and ask Juan to write down a score between one and 10, next comes the Eccles cake. I take a bite out of it but don't like it much, it's slightly greasy and not a very pleasant texture. It might be that I've got cheap ones that have been sitting on the supermarket shelves for ages, but it's not nice. The cheesecake is much better, all creamy and delicious, but the topping is a bit tart, making it difficult to eat. Both Juan and I scrape the black-currant topping off and eat the cheesecake underneath with gusto. I give it 6 out of 10, having awarded Victoria sponge five and Eccles cake four. The chocolate cake is really lovely, and earns itself 7 out of 10 for its chocolatey gooey loveliness. Following that the lemon drizzle cake is surprisingly lovely and I eat the whole lot up. I have given the chocolate cake eight and the lemon drizzle cake seven. I turn to Juan and look at the numbers he's written down. His writing is barely legible, but I can see that he's given chocolate cake 12 out of 10 and lemon drizzle cake 46. The first two cakes are in the minus numbers and cheesecake just has a picture of a house next to it.

"It looks like you've chosen chocolate cake and lemon drizzle cake which are the two that topped my table as well."

"Yes," he says, "I really like the cheesecake though maybe I'll vote for that instead of lemon drizzle cake."

"But you've given lemon drizzle cake 46 out of 10."

"Yes, because I liked the topping on the lemon drizzle cake, but I didn't like the topping on the cheesecake."

"Me neither, so I suggest the chocolate cake and lemon drizzle cake go through to the next round with chocolate cake in the first place. What do you think about that?"

"I think we should all drink more wine," he says, raising his class. That boy clearly does not drink enough normally, I've drunk the same amount as him and I'm way more sober.

"So, ladies and gentlemen, please come back tomorrow for group B, the competition takes place at 1 pm, and it's between fondant fancy, fruit cake, gingerbread cake, Jaffa cakes and coffee and walnut cake. See you tomorrow."

# CHAPTER FIVE

*A*s soon as we come off air, I get a text from Charlie: "Well done, that was so funny. Looking forward to tomorrow. I got quite into it in the end!"

"Well, we've got at least one view," I tell Juan. "Shall we have a look at how many other people were gripped by the World Cup opening round?"

"Yes," says Juan, from his position on the floor, where he has collapsed in an undignified heap: the pressures of too much alcohol, dying my hair ginger and hosting a World Cup tournament have proved far too onerous for him. "It should say below the video how many views we've got."

I go to our YouTube page and take a look. One view. Really? "Just one person watched," I say to Juan. "I wonder who that person was, though. It could have been someone really influential in the international cake community."

"No, sweetheart. That will have been Charlie, remember."

"Oh."

Damn. After all that, Charlie was the only person to watch it.

"Never mind," said Juan. "We had good fun. Spending the whole day drinking wine and eating cake must have pleased you. I should eat something that's not cake before going to bed though. Shall I make us something nice? Chicken stir fry?"

"Yes please," I say. "And another glass of wine."

As soon as I say it, I realise that I should also have a glass of water. I've resigned myself to the fact that my alcohol consumption has spiralled out of all control during lockdown, but I should definitely drink lots of water as well.

I always have a real dilemma when it comes to water, though, because I like filtered water, and I keep it in a jug in the fridge. Over time, the jug gets a bit gunked up with hard-water deposits. I did some research on google to find out how I could avoid this, but the only advice that the blessed Google gave was to fill the jug using filtered water. To achieve this, I would need to acquire another filter jug. In time, this will become gunked up. To avoid this, I'll have to fill it with filtered water from another jug. I don't know whether my cupboards are big enough for all the jugs I'll need to purchase just to have a nice glass of water. I also think it will take up all my wages, and severely limit the amount of cake I'll be able to afford.

"Juan, can you bring me a glass of water," I say. "Just tap water is fine."

"Here you go," he says, passing me wine and water. "I was just thinking: do you think we ought to eat just a slice of each cake tomorrow. A small piece each instead of demolishing half the cake?"

"No," I say. "That's irresponsible. We have made a commit-ment to judge the cakes in a major international tournament and we should eat plenty in order to judge them properly. The more you eat the better position you are in to assess them."

"Fair enough," says Juan. He is never very argumentative when he's drunk: he just agrees with everything. I'm the same. We pretty much drink a lot then sit there in quiet contemplation before telling one another how much we love each other, then go to bed. It's a fine arrangement, to be fair. "After supper, do you fancy doing some keep fit with me? You did promise."

"I'm a bit tired today," I say. Perhaps tomorrow?"

"OK," he agrees. "Let's exercise tomorrow."

Five minutes later, with the stir fry burning on the stove, he's fast asleep, snoring gently while the 10 O'clock news bongs into action on the television and a surly newsreader prepares to tell us that lots of people have died today.


Next morning I am up early, and have put the next five cakes on display, ready for Group B of the *World Cup of Cakes* ™ before Juan is even awake. We know how YouTube works now, so putting up the video shouldn't be such a drama. I'm going to try really hard not to get hammered, then nothing can go wrong.

Once the cakes are out and looking ready for assessment, I take Juan a cup of tea in bed.

"We mustn't drink so much when we are doing our cake tasting today," he says, as soon as I walk in the door.

"Don't worry," I say, handing him the tea. "I was thinking just the same thing. But don't call it 'cake tasting' like we are little old ladies at the village fair. This is the *World Cup of Cakes* ™. This is big-time."

"You are funny," he says, sipping his tea and winking at me. I sit down on the end of his bed and pull out my phone, looking to see whether we have any more views.

"We've got three now!" I say to Juan. "I mean, I know it's a slow start, but we've trebled our viewership over the day. That's not bad, is it?"

"No. Except, those two additional views are probably us two looking at the video last night."

"Oh yeah. Damn. That's a shame. I wonder how we get more views. I'm going to investigate."

As with all modern investigations, I just asked Google.

"Hashtags," I say to Juan. "They will be the answer to all our prayers."

"And what are they when they're at home?"

"Well, funny you should ask," I say, reading from the explanation on my phone. "They are when you put a word in the description of the video, with a hashtag in front of it, then anyone interested in that word, will find your video."

"Say that again, I didn't understand a word of that."

"OK, so our video is about cakes, yes?"

"It is indeed."

"So, people interested in cakes might go in to YouTube and put #Cakes and that way they will be able to find any videos about cakes."

"Oh, hashtags. Yes, of course we should have hashtags."

"What did you think I was saying then?"

"I thought you said hash fags."

"Hash fags?"

"Yes. Some terrible drugs. I thought we had to smoke hash fags to get more views. I was confused. It's early. Carry on..."

"Well, that's it, really. We need to go back to that first video and put lots of hashtags in the description that are searchable, then we need to do hashtags before we post this afternoon's video."

While I move into the sitting room and set about adding in hashtags to the first video, Juan does some early morning Pilates, and stretches out before his shower. I'm not sure what hashtags to go for, so I use cakes, obviously, then all the cakes that were in the tournament, and World Cup of Cakes ™, just in case we can get that trending. And some descriptive words like "Yum" and "delicious", as well as some of the toppings that were on the cakes, and words like 'icing', 'cream' and 'jam'.

After that I set about preparing a list of hashtags for today's cakes. We are testing fondant fancy, fruit cake, gingerbread cake, Jaffa cakes and coffee and walnut cakes. This is the most controversial group by far. I am sure there will be an international outcry over Jaffa cakes, and people might also react violently to the inclusion of fondant fancies. We might have to get police protection if things get really out of hand. It is also my least favourite of the groups, if I'm honest. I mean – I love them all – I'm not a monster. But: fruit cake? Gingerbread cake? It's all a bit 'afternoon tea at auntie's house' isn't it? I love coffee and walnut cake though, so looking forward to getting stuck into that.


"Ladies and gentlemen, welcome to the *World Cup of Cakes* ™," I say, smiling warmly into the camera. I've dressed up for day's episode in a loose-fitting satin type top, and with makeup on (make-up! Remember make-up? I haven't worn any for so long I couldn't remember how to apply it at first). The one thing I didn't put on was my bra because one of the great joys of lockdown is the fact that you don't need to wear a bra ever...not even when you're presenting a major international tournament.

"I'm delighted to be joined by my co-host, Juan Pedro," I continue. "Juan? Where are you?"

"Here I am," comes a voice from knee height. For reasons best known to himself, Juan has decided to come crawling into view in a sort of backbend - scrabbling along like a crab. "Hello viewers. Use me as a table," he says.

"Really?"

"Yes, I can be a cake table."

"OK."

Rather unwillingly, I lay out the first cake on Juan's stomach. "The first contender is the fondant fancy," I say, lifting up the bubble gum pink coloured sponge creation and taking a large bite from it. "Mmmmmm...I'd forgotten how delicious they are," (This is not true - I remember exactly how delicious they are because I ate three before the recording started). "How are you going to try it, Juan?"

"Feed it to me. I am a table who can also eat," he says. We've now moved from the realm of the absurd to the realm of the insane.

"Sure." I bend over to feed him, giving all the millions of viewers (well, Charlie, anyway) a shot of my frighteningly large breasts as they sway, free from constriction, inside my loose top. I push the piece of cake into Juan's mouth, still not quite sure how this is going to work, but taking his word at face value, and feeding him nevertheless. He begins to chew on it nodding from his bizarre subverted position. Then he begins choking, I mean really gasping, coughing and spluttering. Bits of sponge and bright pink icing fly out all over the laptop screen before he collapses into a heap, rolling onto his side and coughing like a lunatic.

I drop to my knees and slap his back gently to make sure all the cake is removed. "We'll be right with you viewers. Just hold on there," I say, while Juan continues coughing and I become more and more rigorous in my thumping.

Finally, he calms. The coughing stops and we both look up at the screen which is now covered in bits of pink cake. My face is scarlet with exhaustion and my breasts are practically hanging out of my top. Juan is in a heap on the floor.

"Ladies and gentlemen, excuse that little diversion, we are now back with the second cake in group B. It's the good old fruit cake. Juan sits up on his knees, and I join him on the floor, so we are staring straight into the screen while we eat the fruit cake.

"It's nice and moist, but I'm not a huge fan, I have to say."

"Me neither," he says, between coughs.

We both jot down our scores, and move on to the ginger-bread cake.

"That is terrible," says Juan. "Really the worst cake I've ever tasted."

We both take huge sips of wine, which we hadn't planned to do, but considering Juan almost died in a choking incident and the cake is terrible, it feels like drink is the only way forward.

"Next cake... Jaffa cake," I say, and Juan looks at me sternly.

"I know what all you viewers are thinking... should a Jaffa cake be allowed in a *World Cup of Cakes* ™? This is an issue that we have pondered, and researched, and decided that the Jaffa cake is indeed a cake, because it has cake in the name, and is very cake-like." Juan makes notes as he eats his, taking a second one in before addressing the camera. "It's very nice," he says with a mouthful of orange jelly and chocolate.

The final cake is coffee and walnut cake and, there is no way of hiding this, it's absolutely delicious.

"Well this is my winner," I say to Juan, as he scrapes some of the icing on the top and licks it.

"It really is delicious," he says. "I love this one."

It doesn't take much for us to decide that coffee and walnut cake is the winner and, rather controversially, Jaffa cakes go through in second place.

"I know, I know, purists amongst you will still feel the Jaffa cake shouldn't be in this tournament, but they are in the tournament and the rules of the tournament state that the judges' word is final. We think they should go through in second place and so they will. Thank you everyone so much for watching today. I'm sorry that Juan the table collapsed and nearly died, and I'm sorry that you were forced to watch a screen covered in pink splashes of icing, but besides that I hope you all enjoyed the competition and look forward to seeing you back for the next matches. For those of you who aren't aware, Group C is the group of death. See you at 1 pm tomorrow."

As we finish the broadcast, Juan downs his glass of wine and coughs again.

"What possessed you to think that you could eat a fondant fancy white upside down in a bridge?" I ask.

"I don't know. If I'm completely honest I've no idea why I came crawling in like a bridge in the first place. I just thought it might be fun."

He sits up as he talks to me and I give him a great big hug. "It was fine. It was perfect," I say. "The best World Cup of Cakes there's ever been."

"So, shall we do some fitness work now then?"

"Perhaps a bit later," I say. "I just need to clean pink fondant fancy icing off my laptop screen first."


I manage to avoid any unnecessary exercise for another day, though I strongly suspect that Juan will tire of my excuses soon. Instead I persuade him to join me on the sofa for some pizza that's been in the freezer for bloody ages (though I don't tell him quite how long it's been there), and more wine.

"Fancy watching 'After Life'?" says Juan.

"It's supposed to be really sad, though," I respond. "I don't want to end up crying."

"Don't be silly. It's comedy: it's Ricky Gervais. It will be lovely. Christ, if you can't watch a programme on television without crying, there's something wrong with you. Come on...have pizza and let's watch."

I think it was on about episode four that Juan broke. His little lip had been trembling like crazy as he watched Gervais's character watch videos of his late wife, then something happened. I won't tell you what, because I don't want to spoil it for you if you haven't seen it yet, but Juan lost it. He cried like a baby, sobbing and sobbing as I tried to cheer him up.

"I don't normally cry but this is breaking my heart," he said. The only thing that stopped him was my mobile ringing and neither of us being able to find it. We jumped off the sofa and pulled all the cushions off until I saw it there, bleeping and flashing at me.

"Hello, Mary Brown," I said. It didn't say who the caller was, and I rarely answer when I don't know who's calling, but I made an exception.

"Hello Mary, it's lovely to speak to you. My name is Patricia Dudley, I'm a journalist from Mail Online. Have you got a minute to talk to me?"

"I am, yes, sure…" I say. "What's this all about?"

"We were just calling you because we saw your fantastic video this afternoon, and all the amazing numbers watching it. We wanted to talk to you about why you decided to do a *World Cup of Cakes* ™?"

"What do you mean, lots of people have been watching it? We only got one viewer, and that's my friend Charlie."

"You need to take a look," said Patricia the journalist. "It was Shared by *PewDiePie* this afternoon, and now it's being shared all over the place this afternoon. It's been trending on Twitter for two hours."

"Oh my God. Oh my God. Juan, our video is trending on Twitter Because of tweedy pie or something?" I say to my heart broken flatmate who is still staring at the screen where Ricky Gervais's tearstained face has been paused mid-cry.

"Is that Juan from the video?" asks Patricia. "The one who came crawling in doing a backbend and tried to eat cake upside down before collapsing? Has he stopped coughing yet?"

"Yes, just about," I say. She proceeds to ask me a whole load of questions about why we decided to do the World Cup. I have drunk enough to answer her honestly, and tell her that I was after an excuse to eat as much cake as possible. She then asks to be handed over to Juan, who tells her all about his Pilates, and that the ginger cake is the worst thing he has ever eaten in his life.

She says it was very funny how seriously we are taking the organisation of the competition, she loves the fact that there are quarter finals and semi-finals.

"Yep, that means we can all eat more cake," I say.

She laughs a lot, and seems to be genuinely very nice. Once we get her off the line, I grab my laptop and open it, looking at the number of views. "900,000 views," I say to Juan, as he drops his tissue and stares at me like I have 14 heads. "How many?"

"Almost 1,000,000 views. Bloody hell."

# CHAPTER SIX

*I* wake up on Thursday morning, stretch and then remember… we are internet sensations! Almost 1,000,000 people watched our video. And I think I did an interview with Mail Online. Or did I? God, I was so drunk by the time she rang I can't remember. Is everyone as bad as me during lockdown? I seem to be getting through the days with a mixture of wine, cake and quiet disbelief at the fact that I'm not allowed outside, and don't have to work.

I grab my phone and head onto the Mail Online page. I scroll down but can't see any mention of us, so I put my name into the search bar. There it is - an interview with me, links to the video, and even the draw for the *World Cup of Cakes* ™ included. It's set out so you can fill-in the winners as the week goes on. Oh my God, this is amazing. I scroll down to the bottom of the article and read a few of the 600 odd comments on there.

"Wow that fat girl's got massive bangers."

"That is the funniest thing I've ever seen. What's with the bloke coming in like a crab?"

Yeah, no. I'm not reading any more of those. I go back up to the top of the article and start to read it. The journalist explains that *PewDiePie* - a massive blogger with millions of followers mentioned in his video that he had been eating a lot of cake in lockdown and asked for recommendations. He then searched #cake while doing his live broadcast, and came across our video. He told everyone to go and watch it because it was the funniest thing he'd ever seen. As the journalist explains, that's how he ended up diverting loads of traffic to us, and giving us such a huge audience.

I decide to search out his *YouTube* videos. Bloody hell, he has hundreds of millions of followers. It's ridiculous. I scrutinise him as he watches our video; he cries with laughter when I bend over in my loose-fitting top. I will definitely wear a bra for today's group stage, and squeals with delight at Juan's antics.

Next *PewdiePie* goes back into the first video we did, and laughs hysterically at that. "Oh, look at this poor guy, he's dyed his friend's hair the same colour as Donald Trump and he's all sad. Oh my God, that's so funny. Perhaps that's why he came in like a crab the next day? To apologise? I love these two. They are hysterical."

I suddenly feel very nervous. Even though I joke with Juan about the huge audience we will get on *YouTube*, I never really believed we would get any more than one or two people watching. I only wanted to do it for a bit of fun, and to eat cake, and while away the days with a bit of laughter. I hadn't expected some *YouTube* Megastar to launch my little cake competition into the stratosphere. Now they are running 'pull out and keep' World Cup tournament plans on Mail Online, and almost

1,000,000 people are waiting for the Group C cake eating contest today.

I open my wardrobe and flick through the clothes in there. What should I wear? Something bright and colourful, but also something a little more sophisticated than yesterday. We also mustn't drink. If we can just stay sober before we do the tournament, we can have a drink afterwards. I pull out a red top and jeans. I put on my makeup, and try to do something with my ridiculous ginger and blonde hair.

I am just holding up some necklaces over the red top when my phone rings. I half expect it to be Mail Online again, but when I answer it, it is a lady called Margaret Banter from the communications department at McVities. She wants to talk to me about the inclusion of Jaffa cakes in the tournament, and to ask me whether we needed more Jaffa cakes sent to us in time for the quarters, semis and final.

"Yes, that would be great. Thank you," I say.

"We would all like to say to you, from McVities, that we are very delighted that you recognised Jaffa cakes as a cake, and we are absolutely thrilled that we are through to the quarter-finals."

"OK," I say, unsure what else to add. I hope this isn't a wind up of some kind. Surely a big company like McVities wouldn't be remotely bothered about whether a fat lady from Cobham likes their biscuits/cakes?

I jump in the shower before making a cup of tea and taking one into Juan, but by the time I get out of the water, there's another message. This time it is from Sara Lee, the cheesecake company. They have watched the first video, and are complaining that we featured a blackcurrant topping on the cheesecake instead of strawberry.

"We just all feel that most people prefer strawberry cheesecake, and if you had featured that, you wouldn't have had to scrape the topping off, and would've had a more enjoyable experience. Can we send you some strawberry cheesecake?"

"Sure," I said. Because of course that's what you say when a stranger rings up and asks you whether you want her to send you a whole bloody pile of strawberry cheesecake. But, again, the whole thing is verging on the insane. There's only one thing to do at a time like this: I decide to check on my potato. I pull out the cutlery drawer, stroke Peter's face, and feel a little better about the world.


"Hello, welcome back to the *World Cup of Cakes* ™. I know we have loads more people watching us today because the lovely *PewDiePie* gave us a name check yesterday, and urged people to come along and watch. Thank you very much Mr *PewDiePie*, and I'm glad you're enjoying the World Cup.

"OK, as most of you realise, today is the big battle: Group C…the group of death."

"Group of death…group of death…group of death," says Juan, jumping into view, waving his arms around, saying "Oooooo. Group of death," in a most unusual fashion.

"It's the big challenge, between sticky toffee pudding, banoffee pie, Battenberg cake, birthday cake and red velvet cake. Who will win in this astonishing group of fabulous cakes? There's only one way to find out… Juan cut the cake."

There is a minor problem while Juan says he can't find the knife anywhere, and has to resort to tearing a piece of sticky toffee pudding off for me. It does nothing to lift the professionalism of the broadcast. But cake is cake whether it is torn apart by a mad Spanish man in red leggings, or cut by the Queen's butler. So, I lift it to my mouth, take a bite, and remark on how absolutely gorgeous it is.

"I'm not sure whether this counts as cake though," says Juan, controversially.

I attempt to stare him into silence, but he's having none of it.

"I feel very strongly that this would be better off warmed up and served with ice cream. Anything that is better warmed up and served with ice cream is not a cake, it's a pudding. I am going to mark it down on those grounds."

"It's a very valid point, but in terms of the taste of it it's quite delicious."

"Oh yes, absolutely delicious," agrees Juan as we both finish our pieces of cake and turn to the next one... banoffee pie.

"I'm not sure about banoffee pie either," says Juan. Honestly, I could punch him...

"It's got pie in the title!" he says, defensively, seeing the angry glare I am giving him.

"Just judge it. It's qualified on merit, just judge it on its taste."

"OK," he says. "It tastes nice, but I'm not convinced it's a cake."

We move onto Battenberg cake and birthday cake, both of which are very nice and legitimately cakes. The Battenberg with its gorgeous marzipan lining, and birthday cake – a far superior version of the Victoria sponge because of its colossal amount of icing and piles of sweets on the top are both lovely, but it's the red velvet cake, the last cake in this group that really lifts our mood.

"Oh, my goodness this is great," says Juan. "The icing is just gorgeous, and that cake is so moist and lovely. This is absolutely brilliant. I cannot see any cake overtaking this."

"I agree with you, Juan. It's lovely, but remember this is just the group stage. There is a long way to go."

"Yes, you're very wise," he says, nodding as he consumes an entire plateful. We then vote, and red velvet cake is the clear winner, with me voting sticky toffee pudding into second place and Juan going for birthday cake. He is making such a fuss about sticky toffee pudding not being a cake that I end up relenting and going with birthday cake too, so the Group C winner is red velvet cake with birthday cake in second place.

We sign off, and high-five one another. "We did that without getting pissed, without me flashing my tits, and without you collapsing in a tremendous heap. Things are really looking up."

"Indeed they are," he says proudly.

"Shall we get drunk now?"

"I thought we might do some exercise. Do you remember you said you would do some fitness work with me today?"

"Yes, yes of course, let's do that later. Let's just have a glass of wine and relax first."

"OK, but just a small one. We can drink it while we work out."

"Really? Are you sure? Wouldn't we be better off working out later when we have more time?"

"What? Time is something we simply are not short of. We have a whole load of time, and should spend just some of it doing a workout. You did promise…"

"OK," I say, fishing around for something to distract him.

"You know what we should do first?"

"What? You're not just delaying things again are you?"

"No, not at all, but I'd really value your expert fashion advice on some clothes I bought and I don't know whether to keep them or not."

He looks up, eyes shining brightly. I knew he'd be interested in looking at clothes. As much as he loves working out, and is keen for me to get involved in his workout classes, he is also very keen on fashion, and would love the idea of being seen as a fashion expert.

"I've got these clothes and I'm just not sure whether to send them back or not. Shall we take a look?"

"Yes, give me a fashion show. Like the fashion show that Carrie did when she moved out of her apartment."

"Oh, I love that," I say, clutching my chest. "Yes, I'll try to bring out my inner Carrie. Shall we have wine first though?"

"Always."

For reasons I can't really explain, we neck a bottle of white wine before I go into my bedroom to begin the fashion show.

I pile all of the parcels onto my bed, and look at them. There is nothing here I need advice on. It will all need to go back. The advice thing was just a bit of a ruse to avoid doing any fitness work. Now I have to go marching out there in ridiculous clothes that are way too small for me, and totally inappropriate for the life I lead, just to pretend I need fashion advice.

I open the first parcel and see the bright pink dress that I ordered last week. This is one of the few that fit me, but looks just like a nighty. The frills on the sleeves and neckline make me look dumpy. I guess if you're a willowy 20-year-old, it would look great with Doc Martens and a leather jacket, but on a fat 30-year-old it looks like I'm getting ready for bed.

I put it on with a pile of necklaces to make it look vaguely attractive, and walk out into the sitting room.

Juan delivers his verdict by laughing hysterically. "Really? You're wondering whether to buy that? It looks exactly like my grandma's nightie."

"That'll be a no then?"

Back in my bedroom I pick up the white cape with floral embellishment all over the back of it. Each flower has sequins in the centre, and they fill the back of the cape. From the front it looks elegant, though with a slightly district nurse vibe. From behind it looks like some terrible Victorian tapestry. There is nothing that's nice about it. I put it over the pink dress and saunter into the sitting room, waiting for more laughter.

"Wow, that's fantastic. You have to keep that. It's lovely."

"Really?"

He can't possibly think that this thing looks nice.

"Really. I even think it makes the pink dress look nice. Maybe you should keep that pink dress after all, and you could wear it with the cape. It would be lovely for so many occasions."

Remind me never to take any fashion advice from Juan, ever. There is nowhere in the world, not any occasion anywhere, where wearing this concoction would be appropriate.

"Thanks for that, I'll try the next one on," I say, rushing out of the room to squeeze myself into the lime green trousers and sky-high pink pumps. I leave the cape on top because it's long enough to cover the front where the buttons and zips are far from doing up, leaving my stomach hanging through the gap, like a sausage has burst open. I look atrocious, but am emboldened by the fact that Juan has no fashion sense. I stride into the front room.

"That is perfect. Why don't you normally wear things like this?"

"It doesn't fit and the colour is too bright." I pull back the sides of the cape to reveal my stomach hanging through.

"OK, well that's not ideal. We really are going to have to do some exercise and get rid of that, then the outfit will be perfect."

I smile at him then turn and walk back into the bedroom to try the next thing on. It's a denim miniskirt, so short as to be obscene. I can do it up, but it's very tight, and I spill over the top. I put it on with a pair of sky-high yellow velvet ankle boots and a black and white jumper that has a very acrylic feel to it, as if it may burst into flames at any time.

I totter back into the front room as elegantly as the 6-inch heels will allow, stand with my hands on my hips facing Juan and smile.

"The skirt is great," he says. "I like you in skirts that are short."

"Do you think?"

"Yes, I think so, let's check it's not too tiny. Turn round and bend over and see whether you're still decent."

I do as he suggests, making a real show as I bend, peering coquettishly over my shoulder at him as I do so, pretending I'm a dancer at the Moulin Rouge or something. Poor Juan shakes his head.

"Nope, it's not going to work, you will have to get one a little bit longer. I can see acres of big white pants."

I walk back into my bedroom, preparing to grab my scissors bag and show him how artistic it is, when there's loud banging on the front door.

Whoever is out there seems particularly keen to get in.

"More parcels?" asks Juan, as I open the door cautiously,

standing back so as to make sure there are 2m between me and the delivery driver (he is called Tony, he's really nice, we are good mates now he's here so often).

But when I open the door it is Dave, my neighbour from downstairs standing there. My beautiful, handsome neighbour who seems to look all the more wonderful having been in lockdown. He is one of these guys who just looks better the less he does with his appearance. He is wearing a white t-shirt, jeans, a face full of stubble and a messy haircut. I just wish I wasn't wearing a tiny denim miniskirt and yellow boots.

"Hi Dave, what do you want? You're not supposed to leave your flat, you know."

"Holy fuck - what's happened to your hair?"

"Is that what you came to say? To mock my hair?"

"No. What I came to say is - you've got to switch off the video," he says, pushing past me without observing any of the government guidelines. He sees Juan standing there. "Mate, you need to switch this off, it's still recording. I've just seen Mary's knickers on my 20-inch TV screen. I'm not complaining, but you know – it's about 1 million people watching you now. You've got to switch it off."

"I did switch off," says Juan, as I hobble like a giraffe into my bedroom to change into something more appropriate.

I come back into the sitting room in an old tracksuit. Juan and Dave are standing there, looking serious.

"It was recording, wasn't it?"

"Yep."

"A million people saw my knickers."

"No. Most of them will have switched off after the World Cup. Not many will have stayed on *YouTube* once you finished," says Dave

# CHAPTER SEVEN

*S*o, Dave is wrong. The evidence that people saw me bending over in a tiny denim skirt and yellow suede boots is quick to arrive. My phone doesn't stop ringing as friends and family contact me to warn me that the video is still running, and has recorded me in flagrante. "I know! And in my worst knickers!" I reply. "I have much nicer pants than those."

I admit that I was marginally more concerned that people will think I wear really big pants all the time than I am about complete strangers seeing them in the first place.

My mother is very distressed by the whole thing, of course. She told Barbara, Margaret and Elaine from the Bridge Club to tune into my channel because I was baking cakes for the world. She completely misunderstood the notion of a *World Cup of Cakes* ™, then was doubly shocked at the drunken display of my bottom. Margaret took it all particularly badly, apparently. I understand why. Margaret is a gentle, unworldly soul and it's the second time she's been subjected to the sight of my enormous bottom. The first time was during my video blog when I got stuck up a tree in South Africa, trying to escape from an ape. In the end I had to be winched down by the Safari guides (who usually use the winch for wounded elephants). The whole thing was captured on camera and posted on to the website.

"Margaret has only just recovered from that," says mum accusatively, as if I am setting out deliberately to shock poor Margaret. "She thought she was going to be watching you make short-crust pastry, and there you were again - showing everyone your knickers."

"I wasn't deliberately showing anyone anything," I explain. "It was a simple error."

"Do you think you would make fewer simple errors if you didn't drink so much?"

Well, yes. It's hard to deny that sort of annoying logic.

Dave is finding the whole thing absolutely hysterical, he can't stop himself laughing every time he sees me answer the phone and be forced into apologies and reassurances: "Yes, I am OK" and "Yes, it is embarrassing but there is nothing I can do."

The three of us head outside at 8pm to clap for the carers...our weekly effort to show the world that we really admire and respect everyone working for the NHS and, indeed, anyone working as a carer in these difficult times.

I really enjoy going out, and waving to the neighbours across the street who stand there with their children. We clap and clap, and bang saucepans with large spoons. You can usually hear fireworks going off somewhere, it's quite a performance. The trouble is, no one knows when to end it. It's a bit like Stalin's Russia: no one wants to be the first to stop clapping. The only difference is that in Russia the first to stop clapping for the leader was imprisoned for 10 years; here you're just left with a dismal feeling inside that you have somehow let the NHS down, and all the doctors and nurses who are working so hard.

Some Thursdays I wonder whether we'll ever be able to stop, or whether we'll end up clapping long into the night until, ironically, we need hospital treatment on our poor, bruised hands.

"Are you making any money from these videos," asks Dave, as he follows me back inside. I assumed that he would head off to his own flat after the weekly clap since it's right there...directly in front of us. "Your videos are being seen by a million people; you should be coining it in."

"Should I? How would I do that?"

"I don't know, you should google it though. That *PewDiePie* guy is worth millions."

"I'm going to have a bath," says Juan, once we're all back through the door. "I'll leave you to work out whether we can make millions from this."

Juan disappears off to the bathroom and Dave and I sink into the sofa with our glasses of wine. "Do you want some cake?" I ask. "We've got plenty here."

"No cake for me, thanks," he says as my phone bleeps again to indicate another message. "Why don't you turn the volume down on that thing so you don't have to answer calls from people ringing all evening to say they've seen your knickers. Now get comfortable and let me massage your shoulders. It must be stressful being a superstar. All that fame and potential wealth."

"Don't joke," I say. "It is quite stressful thinking that almost 1,000,000 people are watching you."

"*Almost* 1,000,000? It was almost 1,500,000 when I was

watching you cavorting round in all those clothes you bought. By the way, don't take any fashion advice from Juan, those clothes were all terrible."

"I know, they are all going back, I only suggested that we should do a fashion show to stop him from making me do exercise."

Dave starts kissing my neck and playing with my hair. Oh God, it feels so nice. "Why don't I stay here tonight, and make you feel really good," he says. He starts kissing the side of my face, working his way round towards my mouth.

My God, reader, I know I should push him away but just look at the man. Are you going to turn down that big hunk of manly beauty? No you're bloody well not. I will have to go and change out of these enormous white knickers first though.

"Shall I stay?" he says, gently stroking the back of my neck.

"Yes," I'm about to whisper when the door swings open and Juan walks in wrapped in the tiniest of towels.

"Are you still here?" he says, in a very territorial manner.

"I was thinking of staying the night actually," says Juan.

"Why? You only live about six paces away from us, why don't you go home and sleep there."

"I forgot my keys," he says, suddenly. There had been no mention of this before.

"How convenient," says Juan. I can't believe how aggressive he is being. He likes Dave, but I guess he just thinks Dave staying the night is going to result in all sorts of trouble, and you know what - he's absolutely right.

"OK. You can stay in the spare room and I'll sleep on the sofa."

"There is no need for that," says Dave. "I'll sleep on the sofa."

"No, it's alright, I like sleeping on the sofa," said Juan. "You go in that room. Go on - off you go."

Dave looks horrified. He's not sure what to do though, having mentioned having no keys (which we all understand to be a lie) he can't go home, but Juan is not going to let him sleep in the sitting room from where he could easily sneak into my room. To get from the other bedroom to me, he's got to go past Juan, which is exactly the plan that Juan is making.

"OK then, good night all," says Dave, giving up on the idea of a wild night with me rather too quickly for my liking. He stands up and trails his hand across my breasts as he walks away, across the sitting room towards the bedroom.

"He's a shark," says Juan. "I'll get some sheets and duvets and sleep here; you go to bed and I'll see you in the morning."

"But it's only about 9 o'clock, I'm not going to bed yet," I say, reaching for my phone. When I look at it, I've got about six missed calls. "Oh God, I forgot I turned the sound down. I've got a whole pile of messages in the last 10 minutes."

I go through them one by one and then look up at Juan abruptly. "You won't believe this but Good Morning Britain want to film us for the show tomorrow. Apparently Piers Morgan loves the *World Cup of Cakes* ™, they are sending a camera crew who will interview us on the doorstep in the morning."

"Oh my God," says Juan. "What will I wear?"

"Don't worry. You look lovely in everything."

"But I want something new and dramatic... I'll have to have a think. What time are they coming?"

"I'll find out now."

I reply to the producer by texting the number she phoned on, and telling her that we are willing to go on the show tomorrow. She says that the cameraman will turn up at 7:30am, and they will broadcast either from the doorstep, or inside if we can work out a way of doing it with 2m between us and the cameraman. "OK," I reply.

My life has just taken a very big step into the surreal

# CHAPTER EIGHT

*I* couldn't sleep last night. It's all too odd. My phone was bleeping away long into the night, with texts and WhatsApp messages from friends and work colleagues letting me know that they will be watching my *World Cup of Cakes* ™ tomorrow. Every single one of them mentions that they saw me bending over in my short skirt, or says they saw the first video when I flashed my boobs at the camera. I hate the fact that I do these ridiculous things. I didn't wear a bra in the first video for the simple reason that nobody is wearing a bra in lockdown, surely? And that is just a mistake in the final video...neither Juan nor I realised that the video was still taping us. Thank God Dave turned up. But doubly thank God that I didn't end up sleeping with him. That was so odd back there...the way he started coming on to me. I know this is a terrible thing to admit, but it was quite nice. I'm glad that Juan was there to stop it going further, but also quite disappointed at the same time. Do you know what I mean? It would've been such fun to jump into bed with him, but I know I would feel horrible this morning. Anyway, it didn't happen, and today I'm on the Piers Morgan show. Well, not the Piers Morgan show, it's called Good Morning Britain, but you know what I mean.

First, though, I'm going to have my breakfast on the steps outside just to get a bit of fresh air. In case you're wondering, I'm having a packet of cheese and onion crisps. It's not conventional; I appreciate that, but these aren't conventional times. We're all stuck in a bizarre world; nothing feels real. Normal rules don't apply. In many ways this is a horrible thing...I'd love to go out to the pub, catch up with Charlie and have a good time, but I can't. In other ways it's great, because while there are suddenly lots of new rules about not leaving the house and standing 2 metres away from everyone, the old rules have stopped. They have been furloughed. There's no rule anymore about getting up in the morning, you can stay in bed all day if you want. You don't have to have breakfast at breakfast time and there's really no need to have lunch before 6pm. You can swap the order of the meals round, have them all together or just eat breakfast for every meal in lockdown; no one cares anymore. No one cares if you just eat crisps. So I am.

It's a nice warm day, so I head down the stone steps outside my door to the tiny garden patio and sit on the chair that Juan has placed there to rest his legs while he watches the birds. It's so quiet and peaceful. I can see why he comes here, watching over his flock. I try to look for the birds he's mentioned; Bertie and Winston. I can see some birds, but how am I supposed to know whether they are the right ones? It's probably very birdist of me to say this, but they all look the damn same. He's put some food out of them, on the wall, but they don't seem to have touched it. I'm not sure what food it is, it doesn't look like bread.

There's a bus stop just a few feet from my gate where the number R68 stops. That's the bus that I get to work. I don't know how frequently it's going these days, but there's just one woman waiting where normally there would be a fairly long line at this time of the morning, full of people hurrying to get to work on time.

I nod at the woman and we exchange shrugs and smiles to indicate the surreal situation we find ourselves in. "At least the weather's nice," she says.

"Yes, things are so much better when the sun shines," I agree.

It is a lovely day but there's quite a breeze and the weather forecast suggests we're in for lots of rain and wind later which is a bit of a pain.

I open my crisps surreptitiously so she can't see my odd breakfast choice. It occurs to me that the bizarre rules of lockdown only exist because no one can see you doing things. As soon as there's a spectator from outside my family, I feel as if I ought to slip back into appropriate behaviour. I look over at the woman...she seems nice enough but she has a

long, judgmental face which is quite unnerving...and she is just staring at me, which is doubly unnerving. I look out at the birds in the tree while trying to take one of the potato treats out of the packet, when I drop the newly-opened bag of crisps and a gust of wind blows them across the tiny courtyard and onto the main path. I stoop to recover the packet, but another gust sends it skittering down the path. I then make the fatal decision to pursue it. This is partly because the woman is watching me and might think I am littering the neighbourhood, and partly because I want the damn crisps. Each time the bag seems within reach, another gust sends it tantalisingly away. Thus, I chase it along the path and out onto the main pavement under the direct, unwavering gaze of the woman. There is a trail of crisps to mark the bag's journey, while I stand in the road, in my nightie, looking at the packet which is now right next to the woman's feet. There is one crisp left in the bag. I take the near empty packet and for some ludicrous reason, I say: "I meant to do that," to the woman, before wandering off, back into the flat, to hide my head in shame, and get dressed for the rigours of hosting a World Cup tournament.

I have decided to dress conservatively for today's competition. I want to show the world that I'm not a raving exhibitionist, and hopefully give the impression that I am a calm and rational woman with a particular propensity for cake. I go back inside, and tiptoe past Juan who is still fast asleep on the sofa, bless him. Then I have a shower before returning to my room and dressing. There is a gentle knock on the door. "Hello, it's me, can I come in?"

"Of course you can."

He eases the door open and smiles when he sees me. "You look lovely," he says. "I'm afraid that I'm not going to look very lovely today."

"What do you mean?"

"Well, I can't get into my room, can I?"

"Yes, you can - just kick Dave out."

"I've tried to wake him up but he's fast asleep."

I go to the spare bedroom and Juan is right: Dave is lying across the bed snoring like a giant pig. I give him a quick shake but there is no movement at all.

"Dave!" I try, but still nothing. He just snores a little more loudly and rolls over.

"Can I borrow something of yours to wear today?" Juan asks desperately. "They'll be here soon and I don't want to be standing here in my pyjamas."

I can hear the fear in Juan's voice. It's astonishing that someone who is normally so confident and outgoing feels so wrecked by nerves at the thought of going on television.

"It's going to be OK," I say. "There's nothing to worry about."

"That's easy for you to say: you're all pretty and lovely and everyone adores you. I'm just your sad sidekick."

"Juan!!" I shout, making him jump a little. "What are you talking about? You are my greatest friend. I think the world of you, and so does everyone else."

I'm just about to tell Juan that I don't think I have anything that will be small enough for him when I'm distracted by a knock at the door. Who the hell is this now?

I head out into the corridor and answer it to see three men and a camera, standing back on the steps.

They introduce themselves as producers from the Good Morning Britain show, and they ask whether I mind if they come in so they can work out whether the shoot can be done inside or out. "We don't want to compromise your health or safety, but if you wouldn't mind one of us coming in to have a look, that would be helpful."

"Sure," I reply, standing back to allow them through. They are very early, it's a miracle I'm dressed and ready to go.

They walk into the sitting room, while I dive into my bedroom to tell Juan to get a move on.

"Oh Lord, what can I wear?" he asks. He is wearing silk pyjamas, but there is no way he can wear those on screen.

"Just grab a T-shirt and the smallest pair of jeans I've got, and put a belt on them. The guys are in the front room having a look for where we can do the broadcast."

"Oh shit, I haven't done my hair yet," he says.

"Wear a hat," I say, as I walk back into the sitting room.

"This is perfect, if you don't mind us filming in here?" says the older of the three guys. I tell him that I don't mind at all, and the other guys come in from outside: one is a cameraman and the other is apparently a "sound man." Which I take, first of all, to be an assessment of his character, but then realise it means that he is the one who controls the volumes and sound being transmitted to the studio.

"I'm sorry this is all such a rush," said the producer. "But we absolutely loved your *World Cup of Cakes* ™, and Piers thought it was such a good idea. We're going to try and go live in 10 minutes, is that OK?"

"OK, what sort of questions will you ask me?" I say.

"Piers will be asking the questions from the studio, but I imagine he will want to know why you decided to do it, and what you think about the sudden fame you've got because of it."

"I haven't really got any fame," I say. "I mean, I haven't been out of the house since, so I don't know, but I wouldn't imagine anyone would recognise me."

"They might after you've been on the program," says the producer, as he tries to reach the studio on his phone. "On-air in 7 1/2 minutes," he says to me.

"Yes, that's fine," I say.

I run over to my bedroom door and knock on it. "You need to be out here in five minutes, we're going to be on live then," I say to Juan.

There is a small shriek from the depths of my bedroom. "Everything is too big for me," he says.

Surely this can't be the first time he's noticed that I'm twice his size?

"OK, we are live in three, two, one…"

As Piers Morgan introduces the "next slot, live and exclusive on Good Morning Britain," Juan emerges from my bedroom. I've never seen anything quite like this. Unable to cope with going on air in my size 18 jeans, he has stayed with his silk pyjamas, but covered them up with the Cape I wore yesterday. On his feet he has the sky-high pink shoes, forcing him to hobble and stagger as he walks through the sitting room towards me. Most alarmingly of all, he's decided to put on some of my lipstick. I don't have anything against men wearing lipstick, but it's always a good thing if at least some of it is on the lips and not just smeared around the mouth and chin. It looks like a three-year-old has done it for him.

"Good morning, ladies and gentlemen. Mary and Juan, can you hear me?"

"Yes we can, Piers," I say in my friendliest way, as if Piers and I have been friends for all time.

"Oh my goodness, Juan, you're wearing the cape from yesterday's *YouTube* video."

"Yes, there's a man in my room, so I can't get in there. I have to wear Mary's clothes."

I glare at Juan. "What the hell?" I mouth under my breath at him.

"Ah, OK, well we don't want to know any more about your private life, Juan. I'm glad you're having a good time. Mary, tell me about this *World Cup of Cakes* ™. I understand it was your idea?"

"Excuse me," Juan butts in. "It's not my lover in that room, it's Mary's. I had to separate her from him and so I put him in my room."

What the hell is he doing? Has he lost his mind?

"No, he's not!" I say. "He's not at all - please don't listen to him."

"OK, OK," says Piers. "So, we have two people having a fun time with a male guest. Now, tell us about this World Cup."

"You've made it sound so much worse than it is. No one had fun with the guest. The guest is just a friend; that's all."

"Tell us about this competition then?" he says.

"Yes. The *World Cup of Cakes* ™ started because I'm a real food fan, and I was joking to Juan that I had tried just about every biscuit in the world, and was now going to go onto cakes. I only said it for a joke, but then when I was working out what cake to buy, and wondering which were the best cakes...that's when I decided to host a World Cup tournament."

Piers is laughing in the studio. "I did enjoy it, Mary. I love the seriousness with which you presented it."

"Well, cake eating is a very serious business," I say.

Juan hovers by my shoulder. "I'd just like to say that if my boyfriend is watching, the man in my room is not for me, he's for Mary."

"It's the final group games today," I say to Piers, desperate to edge Juan out of the conversation. I know he's got a new boyfriend, and the lockdown has prevented them from seeing one another, and he doesn't want his boyfriend to know there's been a strange man in the house, but he is throwing me right under the bus in the process, just when I'm hoping to get back with Ted.

"Yes, the final group games today," I repeat.

"I'm looking forward to this final group. I'm a big fan of Christmas cake. How do you think that will do?"

"I'm expecting a good performance from it today," I say, like a sports presenter, introducing the runners and riders before the Grand National. "Obviously, the relationship between icing and marzipan is crucial, as is the moistness of the cake itself. Too little marzipan or too little icing and it doesn't have a chance in a tough group like this." Piers is laughing in the studio, and telling me he loves the way I talk about the cakes.

One of the things you're also famous for in your videos is having a drink or two. Do you think it's important to have wine with cake?"

"Yes, during the lockdown I think that is vital," I say. "Tea and cake are lovely, but when there is a lockdown on, I think you need to up the ante and get the wine open."

Piers laughs and the guys filming me laugh, and I smile dreamily into the camera, and it feels as if this whole interview is suddenly going much better. Then I hear a creak of the bedroom door opening, and out walks Dave in all his masculine glory. Hairy chest, hairy legs and the tiniest briefs as he stomps across the room and stops suddenly next to me, realising I'm on film.

"What the fuck?" he says, backing away and running back into his room.

"He's not with me!" shrieks Juan.

"He's just a friend," I say to Piers. "A friend who lost his house keys and had to stay the night."

"Oh yes, one of those friends." says Piers, chortling with laughter.

"Not my friend," says Juan. "Mary's friend."

The film crew in the flat are smiling to themselves, as Piers puts on a more professional face in the studio:

"Well, we have to go to a break now, so we will leave it there, but good luck with the group matches today. And we have a question for you: can we broadcast the final live on Good Morning Britain on Monday morning?"

"Yes, of course you can." I say.

"Great, we will come back to you then. Juan and Mary - many thanks. Have a lovely weekend with your 'guest' and we will see you on Monday. Everyone else, we will be back after the break…"

"My life is over," said Juan. "Gilly will think I have taken a lover."

"No, he won't," I say. "He might wonder why you're dressed in a ridiculous Cape, silk pyjamas, high-heeled pink shoes that are too small for you, and lipstick, but after everything you said there, I'm pretty sure he knows that you haven't taken a lover."

"I don't think I'm very good on live TV. I'm not going to do any more television."

He limps away, kicking off the pink shoes before going into my bedroom and shutting the door behind him.

I switch my phone back on and brace myself for the stream of texts. I look at mum's first.

"Margaret says she's not going to watch you on TV again."

Then a text from Keith, my boss at work: "Aren't we all supposed to be in lockdown? What are you doing with a strange man in your flat?"

Oh sod this, I'm having a drink.

# CHAPTER NINE

$\mathcal{T}$he next morning Juan is in a better mood, so I persuade him to come with me to buy the final five cakes. I only bought 15 on my first trip, and another five are needed for the final group stage at 1pm today. He's taking an absurdly long time to get ready, then finally appears in yellow trousers and a black and yellow striped jumper. He's half bumble bee; half chick. He looks tense though, as if he's just been asked to come up with a solution to all the world's problems.

"I can't find my sunglasses," he says. "They are nowhere to be seen."

"Don't worry; it's not that bright anyway," I say. "You don't need them. They'll probably spend most of their time on top of your head."

"I hate to wear sunglasses on my head like that," he says. "There are always problems."

"Problems? What sort of problems." We start our walk to

Tesco's without the glasses as he explains why he always wears them on his nose or puts them away in their case, but never wears them on the top of his head.

"Because sooner or later I will forget they are there and go to the toilets, and while I am attending to my business, the glasses will drop from my head into the toilet, and I will piss all over them."

"Fair enough," I say. That strikes me as a perfectly good reason not to perch sunglasses on the top of your head.

As we walk along, I think about how we've all started to appreciate 'outside' a lot more since lockdown. It seems a far more wondrous and exciting place than it did before; full of real-life people and lovely flowers bathed in sunshine. The beauty of nature seems as if it has been lifted from art: more vivacious, bright and beautiful than I recall it being before we were all barred from experiencing it more than once a day.

Today is no exception. I make Juan take the long route to Tesco's which involves us walking by the river for a stretch of it. There we see two handsome male mallards, their necks shimmering with green iridescent loveliness in the sunlight; and, between them, a sweetly demure female in a million shades of brown. When I think of brown, I think of chocolate brown (unsurprisingly), but the subtle blend of browns: from bronze and beige through pine to cinnamon, chestnut and oak is beautiful and uplifting.

"I love nature," I declare to Juan.

"Me too," he replies. "That is why I like to sit out and feed my birds every day."

"Oh, I meant to say, they weren't eating whatever you put out for them yesterday morning, it was still sitting on top of the wall."

"Oh yes - they ate it in the end," he says.

"What was it?"

"It was an old potato that I found."

"A potato?"

"Yes, strangely it was sitting in the cutlery draw, so I chopped it up and fed it to them."

Poor Pete the potato. Still he had a more worthwhile existence that if he had stayed lying in the street.

We turn into the road which leads past the church to the High Street. The first shop we walk past is Oxfam. Juan thinks it's a horrible idea to buy people's second hand 'junk' but I'm quite partial to it, and always like to take a look in the window. Today there's a deflated gym ball sitting there, still in its packaging. Presumably it was handsomely blown up originally, but when the shop closed it has been left there, deflating a little every day. There's something very sad about it. But then I see the geometric lettering on the box has made the word 'GYM' look a lot like the word 'BUM'.

"Bum ball," I said to Juan with a snorty laugh. He doesn't laugh at all, so I try again, saying 'Bum ball' in a loud American accent. Still no effect. Finally, I try it in a French accent. Nothing. So, I look round, wondering what on earth is wrong with him and realise that Juan isn't there. There are just the other passers-by, trying to ignore the odd woman saying 'Bum ball' over and over again, in different accents.

I spot Juan a little further down the street, looking into the barber's window with a wistful look on his face.

"Come on, let's go and get these cakes before I get sectioned," I say. "If you want a haircut before we go on air this afternoon, I'll do it for you."

"It's fine," says Juan, blowing hair up from his eyes. "I will wait until they open. I don't want it ginger."

We manage to buy all the cakes that we need without any hassle. I had been slightly concerned that we would get there to discover the stock had been depleted and we had no way of getting hold of the necessary sponges, but Tesco's did us proud, and we were soon heading back, laden with cakes for the final stage of the group section of the tournament.

As we approach the front door, I can see a pile of parcels gathered outside like people waiting to go inside. Juan sees them too and turns to me aggressively.

"What have you ordered now?"

"What do you mean?"

"You know you've been buying all this rubbish on the Internet? Well take a look...six boxes on the doorstep."

"I bought a brooch," I say. "That's all."

I think everything else I ordered has already come, but I ordered this brooch and then realised afterwards it was coming from China, so it'll probably take ages to appear.

"What about all this lot then? I think you might have ordered more than just a brooch."

"Is this all for me?"

I am fairly sure that it can't be, because I know deep-down that a brooch is the only thing I am waiting for, but the daft thing is, I have been ordering so much, that I can't be sure.

"They have all got your name on them."

Juan has his hands on his hips like an angry school teacher as he speaks.

"Less of the judgement please," I say, reaching for a pair of scissors. He stands there while I score down the packing tape. I don't want him to hover around me in case it is more 'stuff' that

I've ordered...I could do without the look of horror on his face when I pull out shoes with cow faces on them or a handbag shaped like a piece of cheese.

But no! I'm not going mad. That's a relief. Inside the first box is a dozen or more of cupcakes with a letter on the top urging me to allow cupcakes into the next World Cup. It states that the cakes are extremely popular, versatile and tasty. "We appreciate that the tournament rules state clearly that no correspondence will be entered into, and we respect that stance, so we do not expect a reply, but we would be grateful if you would consider our plea, and enjoy these cupcakes."

"Wow," I say to Juan. "Do you think there's cake in all these boxes?"

We open them all with feverish speed to discover that most of them are, indeed. cakes. McVitie's has sent us a range of their finest products, including about 24 boxes of Jaffa cakes, ginger cake and chocolate cake. Juan steps back in disgust at the sight of the ginger offerings.

"Oh wow - look at all this."

The next box has 24 bottles of wine in it: 12 red and 12 white. There is also a box of champagne and a box full of strawberry cheesecakes from the communications executive who had contacted us earlier in the week to express his annoyance that we had blackcurrant topping.

"You know what we should do...take this to a food bank," I say.

"Maybe keep the alcohol?"

"Yes, let's keep the alcohol and give over all the cakes."

"Good plan," says Juan. Then we look at one another because we have no idea how to get boxes and boxes of cakes to a food bank during lockdown. You know this is one of the hardest things about lockdown...normal things suddenly become very difficult. Can we order a taxi? We don't really know. Is it wise to get a taxi? We don't really know. Are all the buses running? Probably? Do they go to where the food bank is, and how on earth would we get all these boxes onto the bus? We just don't know.

"We could ask Dave to give us a lift?" I say. "He owes us after barging trouser less into our broadcast."

"Yes, let's do that," says Juan. "Text him now and ask him if he's free later, and we can do it after the broadcast of the final group stages."

Having settled on this plan, and having texted Dave, we go in and prepare the cakes ready for competition.

We are getting much better at the broadcasts now. We know how to set the whole thing up, and we are quicker at flying through the tasting, giving comments on each piece of cake and then quickly getting to our scores. We also manage to go through the whole thing without me showing any part of myself that should remain covered up, and no naked hairy man emerges in the background. All in all, a complete result.

The cake which wins the group is red velvet cake, knocking Christmas cake into second place. The Christmas cake is unlucky to be in such a tough group, because it is delicious: the absolutely perfect balance of constituent parts. The cake is moist and falls apart in our mouths and the icing is a sugary delight. Marzipan is just the greatest invention ever, anyway, and it absolutely lives up to all expectations. But the worthy winner is red velvet cake. What a joy that cake is. Really, really lovely. At the end of the broadcast, I thank the company that sent us lots of cake, and thank all the viewers for watching us. I remind everyone that the quarter-finals are being held tomorrow, Saturday, the semi-finals are on Sunday and that the final will be held live during Good Morning Britain on Monday. I also explain that we will be donating many of the cakes that have arrived for us to the local food banks, and hope that those that sent them to us understand that this feels like the best thing to do. We then sign off.

"We're getting quite good at this," I say to Juan. He just nods. He still doesn't like television, and isn't keen on the final being broadcast live. He'll be fine though. I'll just keep an eye on his sartorial choices.

"Come on then, let's go and get these cakes to the food bank. Dave has texted to say he's outside in the car."

"I think we could do with Dave in here to help us carry them," says Juan. "That boy has got muscle on muscle. It'll take us half the time with him."

I text Dave and ask him to come in and help us carry boxes of cake down to the car. He carries about four while we have just one each. As we put them into his boot and onto the back seat of the car, we realise there's not enough room for us all to go, so Juan and Dave agree to take them. As they climb into the car, someone comes up and starts taking photos of them.

"I'm from Mail Online," says the photographer. "They asked me to come down here just to get some shots of you guys taking everything to the Food bank. It's a nice touch. Can I grab a picture or two?"

"Sure," I hear Dave say. "We've got everything in the car now, we're just about to head off."

About 20 minutes later, Juan comes bowling into the flat thrilled with the reaction that the cakes receive. "The woman in the centre was so chuffed," he says. "She was wide-eyed when she saw all the cakes. She told me that lives will be made so much brighter and happier because of what we did today. I feel great. Let's always take cake down there if we have too much."

"Sure," I agree. It's great to see Juan looking so happy. "What did that guy want...the one who was hanging around by Dave's car?"

"He was from Mail Online. He heard on the broadcast that we said we were going to the food bank so he came to get pictures."

"Oh, OK," I say. "We're properly famous now. I bet Dave loved it."

"Oh yes - he was posing up a storm."

"Fancy a glass of wine?"

"Of course. I'm just going to get changed and I'll be back. Shall we watch the rest of the Ricky Gervais series?"

"Will you be able to watch it without crying?"

"I'll try."

"OK then, let's do it. I'll get the wine."

I am sitting on the sofa, trying to find the series on Netflix when Juan comes running back into the room with his phone out in front of him, looking like he's seen a ghost.

"It's a nightmare," he says.

"What is?"

"I've had a text. Bad text. Look…"

Poor Juan can hardly speak he's so thrown by whatever he's seen on his phone. I take it off him and read the text.

"I believed you when you said there was nothing going on between you and Dave. Even though he was in the flat and sleeping in your room, I still chose to believe you. Now you've thrown my trust right back in my face."

Underneath, Juan has written: "Babe, what's the matter. I don't understand what I've done?"

"See Mail Online. You and Dave are all over it."

I grab my phone and call up the Mail's website.

*World Cup Cake comics donate to the needy*

"That's a nice headline," I say. "What's the problem?"

"Check out the photos," he says. I scroll down and see lots of pictures of Juan and Dave together. Then I notice a caption:

*Is this mysterious hairy man from the hilarious YouTube video?*

"Ah," I say, handing my phone over to Juan. "I think you should phone him and explain that Dave's the only person with a car and he lives downstairs, that's why he was there. I'm sure he'll understand if you tell him."

Juan doesn't look at all impressed.

"Why has everything gone so wrong?" he asks.

"It hasn't really gone wrong," I insist. "You ended up with your picture in the paper because you did something good. It's a nice piece. I'm sure he'll understand if you explain properly."

# CHAPTER TEN

*I* wake the next morning to a text from Ted. Ted! As soon as I see his name on the screen I leap out of bed. Why is he texting me suddenly, completely out of the blue? Does he want to get back with me? It is then that I remember...at first it was a vague, fuzzy memory, then it forms more clearly in my mind...I texted him last night. Damn. Alcohol is truly the worst thing ever. I check my 'sent' basket before even looking at the text he sent me. Yep: I sent a picture of a heart. No words, nothing, just a heart. I must have sent it because I was feeling all emotional after watching the pain that Juan was going through. Seeing his misery just stoked my own feelings of sadness about not being with Ted anymore. If it hadn't been for this damn pandemic Charlie would have had her party; I might have got back with Ted and we could be dating by now. Perhaps we would have been in lockdown together. That would have been amazing.

I have resisted contacting him since the outbreak of the

virus, but last night it must have all got too much for me, and I drank a lot. AGAIN. Shit.

I turn to read his message. If I am honest with you, I am kind of putting it off, because I'm worried it will be dismissive and cold and will make me feel horrible.

Despite my fears, his text starts in a nice and breezy tone, and I feel that flush of excitement that goes right through you; you know that feeling you get when someone you like contacts you?

"Hi Mary, lovely to see you doing so well with your *World Cup of Cakes*. It did make me laugh! Also really pleased that you've met someone else... I was never Dave's greatest fan, but if he makes you happy, then I'm happy. Ted."

Nooooooo. Oh God no. For God's sake. I text straight back and put him straight. "Ted, Dave is not my boyfriend. Juan explained at great length that he just stayed the night because he lost his keys. He stayed in Juan's room. There is nothing going on between us."

Then my phone does that thing where the little dots appear to show someone is replying, so I sit there, staring at the screen, waiting for Ted's text. Then the little dots go away and there is no message from Ted.

"Everything OK?" asks Juan, coming out of his room.

"Yes, everything is fine, except that Ted thinks that I'm having an affair with Dave, because he saw him wander out into the middle of the flat in his underpants."

"Oh no, angel. Do you want me to talk to him? I managed to talk some sense into Gilly last night."

"I might see what happens. I've told him that nothing is going on, and - to be honest - it's none of his business what I do in my spare time if he doesn't want to go out with me. But thanks for the offer. Maybe later if I don't get any sort of reply from him."

"You know the fact that he cares enough to be cross is good, don't you?" he says. "If he didn't like you, he wouldn't be bothered."

"He isn't bothered," I say. "He's saying he's happy for me and Dave."

Juan takes the phone off me and looks at it. "He's bothered," he says. "That text has got 'I'm bothered' written all over it."

"Really?"

"Yep. If he wasn't bothered, he wouldn't have texted."

"OK. Well that's something, I guess. I'm just glad we've got the World Cup to distract us. His text has made me feel really rubbish," I say.

"Don't, sweetheart, honestly. I know it's hard but he is definitely bothered. Did you reply to him?"

"Yes, I told him that nothing is going on, but he didn't write back."

"Well, you know he's watching now, don't you, so let's make a brilliant success of these remaining videos."

"Yes," I say, suddenly cheered by the thought that he will be watching me. Even if he's fed up with me, I know he'll be watching.

"What time are the quarter-finals, same time as the group games?"

"Yes," I say. "Our legions of fans have got used to the 1pm starts, let's not confuse them."

"Good thinking," he says.


"Ladies and gentlemen, welcome to the quarter-finals of the

*World Cup of Cakes.* Today we have eight teams competing to win places in the semi-finals that will take place tomorrow. Four cakes will go through today, and have the chance to be crowned World Cup winning cake, while four cakes will go home dragging their sugary tails between their legs, hoping to come back next year sweeter and stronger.

"So, without further ado…let's get cracking: the first quarter final is between chocolate cake, and Jaffa cake. May the best cake win."

The first quarter final is a fairly easy win for the chocolate cake, to be honest. There's little discussion as we lick the thick chocolate icing from our lips and praise the glory of the chocolate sponge. But, to be fair to the Jaffa cake, it did well to get through to the final stages of the tournament considering many would argue that it had no place being in a *World Cup of Cakes* ™ in the first place.

"We should just have a few words from the chocolate cake before we move on to the next quarter-final," I say, turning to the cake: "You must be absolutely delighted?"

Juan just stares at me. I was kind of hoping that he would be the cake and answer in a squeaky chocolatey voice, but he doesn't seem keen.

The next quarter final is between coffee and walnut cake and lemon drizzle cake. I know this will be an almighty battle, because I think coffee and walnut cake is one of the greatest tastes in the world, and lemon drizzle cake is a favourite of Juan's, and Juan has equal voting powers (giving him that was a big mistake). This one might come to blows.

We taste the two cakes and I look at Juan: "I think this coffee and walnut cake is exceptional," I say. The lemon drizzle cake is just plain sponge with a bit of lemon flavouring on it. It's really nothing special. I would even go as far as to say it shouldn't really be in the quarter-final of the *World Cup of Cakes* ™.

"You know, I agree with you," he says.

"You do?"

"I've always been very fond of lemon drizzle cake, but it does taste very bland next to the thick coffee icing on this one. If you prefer coffee and walnut then I'm happy with that."

"Well, ladies and gentlemen, that was very simple. We have a winner. Coffee and walnut cake goes through to the semi-final."

The next quarter-final proved to be a shoo-in for red velvet cake. Poor Christmas cake didn't have a chance with the combination of butter icing and delicious red sponge. And in the final quarter-final, brownie knocked out birthday cake.

"We've seen Christmas cake and birthday cake both get knocked out," I say to Juan, shaking my head. "It's really not been a good day for celebratory cakes, has it?"

"No, there will be a huge disappointment in the royal icing fraternity. I hope they can come back next year better and stronger."

"Indeed." I nod knowledgeably and turn to the camera. "Please join us tomorrow for the semi-finals of the *World Cup of Cakes* ™."


I tidy up after the tasting, then go out to find Juan. He is sitting in the garden, motionless, staring at the birds. He's a modern-day ornithological Dr Dolittle. I watch him as he reaches for his phone to take a picture. The bird looks up, presumably frightened by the sudden movement, but then Juan coos gently and the bird settles down and carries on eating the bread that Juan has tossed across the small patio.

# CHAPTER ELEVEN

*A*nother day, another delivery of parcels. Two pairs of shoes - one the wrong size, one too impractical for me to wear, and neither of which I remember ordering.

I head to my computer to log on and find out what the return procedure is for the shoes, but I'm completely distracted by how filthy my keyboard is. It's got to the stage where all I have to do is turn it upside down and shake it, and voila, there's my mid-morning snack.

It won't do, so I go off to get the mini vacuum cleaner that I use when I can't be bothered to get out Henry the Hoover, and I begin hoovering it - trying to get in between the keys to where the real trouble lies. It's all going quite well until three of the keys are sucked off. Damn. There's a sort of clattering sound as they disappear into the machine's plastic belly.

I switch it off and prepare to perform major surgery in order to retrieve the 'q' the 'w' and the 'e' that have been lifted from the top left-hand corner of the keyboard. I'm pretty sure that I could cope without 'q' and normally I'd be confident of managing without 'w', but not when I'm the main organiser of a world cup. And I know I'll need to use 'e' pretty much every time I type. I need to retrieve them, so I pull the thing apart and tip out the collection of hair, crumbs and toenail clippings gathered inside (I hasten to add that the toe nail clippings do not come from my keyboard - they were already in the hoover before I got started). Nestling in the pile of dirt are two of the letters: 'q' and 'w'. Next, I do some vigorous shaking, accompanied by gently fingering the inside of the machine, getting dust and crud lodged up inside my nails. There. Finally, I find the final key, caught in the linking part between the main vacuum and the little brush. Thank heavens for that. I must stick the keys on properly later. When I go out for my daily walk I'll get some strong glue. But what glue? Everyone in the world knows that using superglue means you just stick your fingers together and create horrible peeling on your hands for days afterwards. Perhaps I'll google it, or I'll ask dad. He always likes it when I ask him questions; I think it makes him feel important.

I sit at my computer and look at the screen. What have I come here to do? I've forgotten now. What was it? I walk into the kitchen to make a cup of tea and hope that my memory will be jolted, when there's a knock at the door. I wait a couple of minutes for whoever's there to back away to a safe distance.

By the time I open it, Tony the delivery driver is back in his van. He waves as me before driving away. On the doorstep there are two boxes of wine. Can there be anything greater to find on one's doorstep? I think not. The note inside says: "Well done on your World Cup of Cakes. This is from all of us at Oxford Landing." They have missed the trademark off *World*

*Cup of Cakes* but besides that the letter is the very definition of perfection.


"Ladies and gentlemen, welcome to the semi-finals of the *World Cup of Cakes* ™." I say, while Juan bangs a saucepan in the background like he does on a Thursday night when we clap for the carers. "This is the biggest battle of sponges the world has ever known. The two cakes that go through to the final today will find themselves live on GMB. I wish all the cakes the very best of luck. And can I say a personal thank-you to the kind people at Oxford Landing who have supplied us with loads of wine."

Juan and I raise our glasses and smile into the camera.

"Now, without further ado, let's get on with the judging. The first semi-final takes place between chocolate cake and chocolate brownie...two very similar cakes, Juan."

"Yes," he says with a wise and worldly nod. "Similar chocolatey tastes, but the textures are quite different; it's going to be interesting to see whether the brownie's crunchier outside and gooier inside proves tastier than the thick icing and soft sponge of the chocolate cake. This could go either way."

I pass Juan a plate with a brownie and a slice of chocolate cake on it and we both try both them.

It's extraordinarily difficult to decide, but we both end up plumping for the same one. We announce to the world that the first cake to go through to a place in the final is chocolate cake. Juan takes up the saucepan again and bangs it with such vigour that I'm starting to get a headache. I take a large swig of my drink.

"OK, now we move on to the second semi-final, between coffee and walnut cake and red velvet cake: two very worthy cakes. I wish they could both go through." Again, we bite into the deliciousness of coffee icing and crunch the lovely walnuts. "That's exceptional, Juan, isn't it?"

"Yes," he says, reaching for his saucepan to bash out his appreciation.

"Not now," I mutter. "Let's taste the red velvet cake."

Just one mouthful of that red sponge and thick, buttery icing and I know that all of the coffee cake's hopes and dreams of success are over for another year. The red velvet has done it for me. It's simply lovely. I look at Juan who is licking the icing off the plate. "Red velvet?"

"It's in the final," he agrees.

"Ladies and gentlemen, the cakes through to the World Cup final are chocolate cake and red velvet cake. The final will be live on GMB at 8am tomorrow morning. May the best cake win! The third-place playoff will be held at 6pm tonight between brownie and coffee and walnut cake. Thank you very much for watching."


"We're almost there," said Juan as we load the dishwasher. "Just the third-place play-off tonight, that no one ever cares about, and the final tomorrow morning then we will have run the first ever World Cup of Cakes."

"I can't believe the final's on GMB. That's so odd, isn't it? This whole week has been surreal."

"The whole of lockdown," corrects Juan.

"Yeah. I'm so glad you're here with me. I'd have hated to have gone through this on my own."

"Yeah, me too," he says. "It's been fun, if a bit bonkers."

"And we've got family games night tonight," I say. "Do you

remember? We promised we'd play games online with my mum and Aunty Susan."

"Oh yes, that'll be fun. Are we doing them on house party?"

"Well, yes, that's the plan, but it involves us getting mum set up on the house party app which won't be easy."

"Ah, don't worry. I can explain to her," says Juan. "I managed to get them on zoom so they could play bridge on there, remember?"

"Yes, I do. I remember you shaking with frustration and threatening to throw the lap top through the window."

By 8.30pm that night, Juan and I have held the play-off match in the *World Cup of Cakes* ™, declaring that coffee and walnut cake is the winner, beating brownie into third place. Now we're attempting to run a family games night and Juan is almost in tears. We've been trying to get mum and Aunty Susan set up so we can play against them on house party. There are lots of fun games on there and it's really simple to set up but - my God - we're struggling.

"No, you leave yours alone, you're in there now," Juan is saying to mum. "I just need to help Aunty Susan, then we can all play."

But mum's not listening. She keeps on pressing things and accidentally joining house parties that are going on that she's not invited to. While Juan chats to Aunty Susan, mum can be heard apologising profusely to people.

I've got her on the landline as well as on house party so I can talk her through things as we go, but she won't stop messing around. I don't know what I was like as a child, but looking after me must have been hellish if I was anywhere near as badly behaved as mum and Aunty Susan.

Eventually we have them both on there and the games can start. Juan looks at me through half closed eyes.

"I deserve the Nobel Prize for Fucking Temper Keeping," he says. "That was the worst experience of my life."

"More wine?"

"I need all the wine," he says.

# CHAPTER TWELVE

"It's World Cup final day," says Juan, stomping into my bedroom, banging on a saucepan.

I've been awake since 5am which is a good job. If he'd come into my room banging that saucepan when I was asleep, he'd have scared me half to death.

"It's quite exciting, isn't it? I'm going to wear all yellow today. You should too."

"No, Juan, we'll look like a couple of lemons. I was planning to wear my red dress. It feels like a red dress sort of event."

"Oh definitely. We'll look fab. They should be here in half an hour, shouldn't they?"

"Yes. I'm glad you seem so happy about it," I tell him. "I thought you didn't enjoy the tv broadcasts."

"No, I don't really, but I had a really lovely chat with Gilly this morning and everything is fine. I'm so relieved."

"Oh good, I'm relieved too," I tell him. "He's a nice guy,

everything will be OK, it's just that everyone's a bit nervy and worried at the moment. I guess it does look a bit bad when you're at the beginning of a relationship with someone and you see that another man is sleeping in his room."

"Yep, I guess. But he was only in my room because I was protecting you. I was trying to be chivalrous. You just need to keep Dave away from me when there are cameras around."

"I will," I tell him. "I'll be your bodyguard."

The crew arrives on time. It's the same guys as before, but this time they are wearing masks, having been scolded by the executive producer when they got back to the studio. I'm sure they are safer with the masks on, but understanding what they are saying is proving very difficult. Luckily, it's not they who are asking the questions, and pretty soon we're put through to Piers Morgan in the main studio.

"You look beautiful," he tells me. "Well done for getting all dressed up for the final. "And Juan - you're looking... colourful. Shall we begin?"

"Yes," I say. "First of all, can I announce that the winner last night in the third-place play-off was coffee and walnut cake, so brownie finished in fourth position, coffee and walnut in third, and now we will find out which cake has won and which is in second place."

"Could you just remind viewers of the two finalists?"

"Yes, of course. We are going to be tasting chocolate cake and red velvet cake."

We eat the chocolate cake first and it's lovely. Of course it is. It's chocolate cake.

"Very delicious. It's a good morning cake," says Juan, taking a sip of his wildly strong espresso coffee while I sip my tea.

"Next, the red velvet cake," I say. I'm aware that when I am announcing anything during the *World Cup of Cakes* ™ broadcasts, my voice becomes very serious and drops a couple of octaves.

"Every time I taste this cake, I'm surprised by just how lovely it is," I say. The icing is so thick and creamy and there's so much of it. It's really lovely.

"OK," says Piers in the studio. "What I'd like you to do now is pull the chocolate cake and red velvet cake into the centre of the table. On the count of three, I'd like you both to point at the cake that you have decided is the best in the world. 1, 2, 3…"

Juan and I both point straight at the red velvet cake. There are cheers from the crew in my flat, and cheers in the studio, then the crew throw confetti up into the air and play Nessun Dorma, like they played in that football World Cup. It's amazingly emotional. I hug Juan and turn to hug the sound man, but realise I'm not allowed to, so hug Juan again.

"That was brilliant," says Piers. "Now, I believe we have something for you."

The producer hands me a replica of the World Cup trophy, with my name on it, then he hands Juan one too. "Thank you so much," I say.

"And a couple of other things," says Piers. "British Airways are offering both of you a two-week holiday anywhere in the world once we're out of lockdown. You can each take a guest. I'm sure you'll want to invite underpants man."

"NO!" we both shout.

"There's also a cheque for £2000 each spending money," he adds.

"Thank you so much," we both say, as they cut to an ad

break in the studio, and the cameraman starts to put away all his equipment.

"Well done, guys. That was great," he says. "Really good. Enjoy your holiday, won't you."

# CHAPTER THIRTEEN

*L*ater that evening, as Juan and I lay on the sofa, thinking about the week we've just been through, and surveying the boxes of wine scattered through the flat, I make an unusual suggestion: "I think we should do that training now."

Juan jumps back like he's just been shot.

"There's no need to look quite so surprised."

"Yes there is - I'd given up asking because you always create reasons why you can't exercise."

"I know. I find it hard, but I really want to try now. As soon as we come out of lock down it's Charlie's birthday party, and I'll get to see Ted. I want to be svelte and gorgeous. Can you help me?"

"We could do a World Cup of fitness exercises," he says, full of joy. "Imagine it...each exercise is rated by us, one after the other...how much fun would that be?"

"No Juan - no more World Cups. I think I'm done with hosting major international tournaments for a little while. Let's just start doing some gentle exercise; you and I, on our own. I'll go out later and buy some healthy food, and let's get gorgeous in lockdown."

"OK, it's a plan," says Juan, as we hear a loud knock on the door.

"Oh lordy, Miss Brown, what have you been buying now?"

"Nothing," I say, raising my palms as a sign of my innocence.

I open the door to see Tony the driver retreating back to his van.

"Boxes there for you, love," he says.

Juan and I open one of the six large boxes; they are full of red velvet cake.

"Tony," I call after the driver. "They are for Dave in the flat downstairs. Do you mind helping us?"

Juan and I laugh to ourselves as we take a box each and Joe carries the rest. We plonk them outside Dave's door, then we rush back up the stairs while Tony knocks on Dave's door.

"Delivery for you, mate," he says, climbing back into his van.

"Thanks," says Dave, his voice tinged with confusion.

"Enjoy!" say Juan and I rushing back into the flat.

"Shall we have a glass of wine before we start our exercise programme," I suggest.

"Oh, go on then," says Juan.

"Actually," I add. Perhaps we should start the exercising tomorrow?"


**Want to know what happens next?**
  **Of course you do!**
  *Adorable Fat Girl and the Reunion* (click here: My Book) tells

the story of what happens when Charlie's party finally takes place. Mary meets up with Ted - her lovely, kind, thoughtful, wonderful ex-boyfriend. She is still madly in love with him, but how does he feel about her? Will love blossom once more? Or has Ted moved on?

Featuring river boats, a wild psychic, a glamorous Spanish dancer named Juan, lots of gossip, fun, silliness and a huge, glorious love story...but is the love story about Ted & Mary or someone else entirely?


UK: My Book
    US: My Book

**BOOK ONE:**

**Diary of an Adorable Fat Girl**

Mary Brown is funny, gorgeous and bonkers. She's also about six stone overweight. When she realises she can't cross her legs, has trouble bending over to tie her shoelaces without wheezing like an elderly chain-smoker, and discovers that even her hands and feet look fat, it's time to take action. But what action? She's tried every diet under the sun. This is the story of what happens when Mary joins 'Fat Club' where she meets a cast of funny characters and one particular man who catches her eye.

CLICK HERE:

My Book

**BOOK TWO:**

**Adventures of an Adorable Fat Girl**

Mary can't get into any of the dresses in Zara (she tries and fails. It's messy!). Still, what does she care? She's got a lovely new boyfriend whose thighs are bigger than her's (yes!!!) and all is looking well...except when she accidentally gets herself

into several thousand pounds worth of trouble at the silent auction, has to eat her lunch under the table in the pub because Ted's workmates have spotted them, and suffers the indignity of having a young man's testicles dangled into her

face on a party boat to Amsterdam. Oh, and then there are all the issues with the hash-cakes and the sex museum. Besides all those things - everything's fine...just fine!

CLICK HERE:

My Book

## BOOK THREE:

### Crazy Life of an Adorable Fat Girl

The second course of 'Fat Club' starts and Mary reunites with the cast of funny characters who graced book one. But this time there's a new Fat Club member...a glamorous blonde who Mary takes against. We also see Mary facing troubles in her relationship with the wonderful Ted, and we discover why she has been suffering from an eating disorder for most of her life. What traumatic incident in Mary's past has caused her all these problems?

The story is tender and warm, but also laugh-out-loud funny. It will resonate with anyone who has dieted, tried to keep up with any sort of exercise programme or spent 10 minutes in a changing room trying to extricate herself from a way too-small garment that she ambitiously tried on and is now completely stuck in.

CLICK HERE:

My Book

## BOOK FOUR:

### FIRST THREE BOOKS COMBINED

This is the first three Fat Girl books altogether in one fantastic, funny package

CLICK HERE:

My Book

## BOOK FIVE:

### Christmas with Adorable Fat Girl

It's the Adorable Fat Girl's favourite time of year and she embraces it with the sort of thrill and excitement normally reserved for toddlers seeing jelly tots. Our funny, gorgeous and bonkers heroine finds herself dancing from party to party, covered in tinsel, decorating the Beckhams' Christmas tree, dressing up as Father Christmas, declaring live on This Morning that she's a drug addict and enjoying two Christmas lunches in quick succession. She's the party queen as she stumbles wildly from disaster to disaster. A funny little treasure to see you smiling through the festive period.

CLICK HERE:

My Book

## BOOK SIX:

### Adorable Fat Girl shares her Weight Loss Tips

As well as having a crazy amount of fun at Fat Club, Mary also loses weight...a massive 40lbs!! How does she do it? Here in this mini book - for the first time - she describes the rules that helped her. Also included are the stories of readers who have written in to share their weight loss stories. This is a kind approach to weight loss. It's about learning to love yourself as you shift the pounds. It worked for Mary Brown and everyone at Fat Club (even Ted who can't go a day without a bag of chips and thinks a pint isn't a pint without a bag of pork scratchings). I hope it works for you, and I hope you enjoy it. CLICK HERE My Book

## BOOK SEVEN:

### Adorable Fat Girl on Safari

Mary Brown, our fabulous, full-figured heroine, is off on safari with an old school friend. What could possibly go wrong? Lots of things, it turns out. Mary starts off on the wrong foot by turning up dressed in a ribbon bedecked bonnet, having channelled Meryl Streep from Out of Africa. She falls in lust with a khaki-clad ranger half her age and ends up stuck in a tree wearing nothing but her knickers, while sandwiched between two inquisitive baboons. It's never dull... CLICK HERE:

My Book

## BOOK EIGHT:

### Cruise with an Adorable Fat Girl

Mary is off on a cruise. It's the trip of a lifetime...featuring eat-all-you-can buffets and a trek through Europe with a 96-year-old widower called Frank and a flamboyant Spanish dancer called Juan Pedro. Then there's the desperately handsome captain, the appearance of an ex-boyfriend on the ship, the time she's mistaken for a Hollywood film star in Lisbon and tonnes of clothes shopping all over Europe.

CLICK HERE:

My Book

## BOOK NINE:

### Adorable Fat Girl Takes up Yoga

The Adorable Fat Girl needs to do something to get fit. What about yoga? I mean - really - how hard can that be? A bit of chanting, some toe touching and a new leotard. Easy! She signs up for a weekend retreat, packs up assorted snacks and heads for the countryside to get in touch with her chi and her third eye. And that's when it all goes wrong. Featuring frantic chickens, an unexpected mud bath, men in loose-fitting shorts and no pants, calamitous headstands, a new bizarre friendship with a yoga guru and a quick hospital trip.

CLICK HERE:

My Book

## BOOK TEN:

### The first three holiday books combined

This is a combination book containing three of the books in my holiday series: Adorable Fat Girl on Safari, Cruise with an Adorable Fat Girl and Adorable Fat Girl takes up Yoga.

CLICK HERE:

My Book

## BOOK ELEVEN:

### Adorable Fat Girl and the Mysterious Invitation

Mary Brown receives an invitation to a funeral. The only problem is: she has absolutely no idea who the guy who's died is. She's told that the deceased invited her on his deathbed, and he's very keen for her to attend, so she heads off to a dilapidated old farm house in a remote part of Wales. When she gets there, she discovers that only five other people have been invited to the funeral. None of them knows who he is either. NO ONE GOING TO THIS FUNERAL HAS EVER HEARD OF THE DECEASED.

Then they are told that they have 20 hours to work out why they have been invited in order to inherit a million pounds.

Who is this guy and why are they there? And what of the ghostly goings on in the ancient old building?

CLICK HERE:

My Book

## BOOK TWELVE

### Adorable Fat Girl goes to weight loss camp

Mary Brown heads to Portugal for a weight loss camp and discovers it's nothing like she expected. "I thought it would be Slimming World in the sunshine, but this is bloody torture," she says, after boxing, running, sand training (sand training?), more running, more star jumps and eating nothing but carrots. Mary wants to hide from the instructors and cheat the system. The trouble is, her mum is with her, and won't leave her alone for a second. Then there's the angry instructor with the deep, dark secret about why he left the army; and the mysterious woman who sneaks into their pool and does synchronised swimming every night. Who the hell is she? Why's she in their pool? And what about Yvonne - the slim, attractive lady who disappears every night after dinner. Where's she going? And what unearthly difficulties will Mary get herself into when she decides to follow her to find out...

CLICK HERE:

My Book

### BOOK THIRTEEN: The first two weight loss books:

This is Weight loss tips and Weight loss camp together

CLICK HERE:

My Book

## BOOK FOURTEEN:

### Adorable Fat Girl goes online dating

She's big, beautiful and bonkers, and now she's going online dating. Buckle up and prepare for trouble, laughter and total chaos. Mary Brown is gorgeous, curvaceous and wants to find a boyfriend. But where's she going to meet someone new? She doesn't want to hang around pubs all evening (actually that bit's not true), and she doesn't want to have to get out of her pyjamas unless really necessary (that bit's true). There's only one thing for it - she will launch herself majestically onto the dating scene. Aided and abetted by her friends, including Juan Pedro and best friend Charlie, Mary heads out on NINE DATES IN NINE DAYS.

She meets an interesting collection of men, including those she nicknames: Usain Bolt, Harry the Hoarder, and Dead Wife Darren. Then just when she thinks things can't get any worse, Juan organises a huge, entirely inadvisable party at the end. It's internet dating like you've never known it before…

CLICK HERE:

My Book

### BOOK FIFTEEN: Adorable Fat Girl and the six-week transformation

Can Mary Brown lose weight, smarten up and look fabulous enough to win back the love of her life?

And can she do it in just six weeks?

In this romantic comedy from the award-winning, best-selling,

Adorable Fat Girl series, our luscious heroine goes all out to try and win back the affections of Ted, her lovely ex-boyfriend. She becomes convinced that the way to do it is by putting herself through a six-week transformation plan in time for her friend's 30th birthday party that Ted is coming to. But, like most things in Mary Brown's life, things don't go exactly according to plan.

Featuring drunk winter Olympics, an amorous fitness instructor, a crazy psychic, spying, dieting, exercising and a trip to hospital with a Polish man called Lech.


My Book


### BOOK SIXTEEN: Adorable Fat Girl in lockdown

This book! I hope you enjoyed it x

### BOOK SEVENTEEN: Adorable Fat Girl and the Reunion


The book opens at an exciting time...our gorgeous, generously proportioned heroine is about to be reunited with Ted - her lovely, kind, thoughtful, wonderful ex-boyfriend. She is still madly in love with him, but how does he feel about her? Will love blossom once more? Or has Ted moved on and met someone else?

Featuring river boats, a wild psychic, a lost dog, a gallant rescue operation by a glamorous Spanish dancer named Juan, lots of gossip, fun, silliness and a huge, glorious love story...but is the love story about Ted & Mary or someone else entirely?


My Book

## SUNSHINE COTTAGE BOOKS

Also read Bernice's romantic fiction in the Sunshine Cottage series about the Lopez girls, based in gorgeous Cove Bay, Carolina.

CLICK HERE:

My Book

-

## THE WAGS BOOKS

Met Tracie Martin, the crazy Wag with a mission to change the world... CLICK HERE:

Wag's Diary

My Book

Wags in LA

My Book

Wags at the World Cup

My Book

Printed in Great Britain
by Amazon

81004004R00068